A Celtic Yuletide Carol

by

Jennifer Ivy Walker

Christmas in the Castle Series

A Celtic Yuletide Carol

Cover Art by *Lisa Dawn MacDonald*

The Wild Rose Press, Inc.
PO Box 708
Adams Basin, NY 14410-0708
Visit us at www.thewildrosepress.com

Publishing History
First Edition, 2024
Trade Paperback ISBN 978-1-5092-5744-7
Digital ISBN 978-1-5092-5745-4

Christmas in the Castle Series
Published in the United States of America

Dedication

To my son Jared, whom we called from the darkness into the light of love

Chapter 1

Le Château de Montmarin

The clamorous din from inside the bawdy tavern shredded the calm of the salty night air as Gaultier went into the Drunken Crow to drag his brother home. As usual, Cardin was passed out on a table in the back of the inn, a mug of ale next to his bloodied fist.

Amongst the strands of long brown hair stuck to the side of Cardin's unconscious head, Gaultier noted the swollen eye, bruises, and dried blood smeared across the bearded face. With a broken table, chair, and shattered glass all over the nearby floor, it appeared that, once again, Cardin had been in a boisterous brawl.

Which meant that Gaultier would have to pay for the damages.

And pick up the pieces of his battered, broken brother.

As he stood at the entrance of the tavern quickly assessing the situation, female servers with platters of savory seafood and pitchers of ale scurried about, weaving between tables where sailors, knights, and fishermen celebrated in raucous revelry. Floating notes of flutes, lutes, and lyres accompanied a troubadour's melodic voice near a crackling fire in the enormous stone hearth along a wooden side wall. The innkeeper—a stout, balding man with a soiled white apron and a scowl

1

upon his florid face—indicated with an impatient jut of his chin the destruction that Cardin had caused.

For which the disgruntled owner expected prompt, generous compensation.

Gaultier strode over to the mahogany bar, handed the portly man a bag of silver, and headed toward the rear of the tavern to rouse his inebriated sibling.

He shook Cardin's shoulder and grabbed hold of his arm, peeling his plastered torso from the wooden tabletop. "C'mon, let's go home. Get you in bed to sleep it off."

Grumbling incoherently, Cardin staggered to unsteady feet, wavy locks adhered by drool, blood, and vomit to the side of his bristled, crumpled cheek. Supported by Gaultier's steadfast grip, he leaned against his older, taller brother's sturdy shoulder, stumbled across the floor, and practically fell out the exit door.

"I'm sick of dragging you out of every tavern in town. I'd rather be at the Sultry Siren, bedding a beautiful wench. Like Dolssa, who's probably waiting for me right now. By the Goddess, Cardin, you have to stop this insanity. Or your gambling, drinking, and bloody temper will get you killed!"

Moonlight reflected off the turbulent ocean as Gaultier half dragged, half carried his younger brother along the narrow cobblestone street from the center of the town of Biarritz, up the steep incline to the stone fortress of *le Château de Montmarin,* perched atop the peninsular promontory overlooking the savage sea.

He missed *la Bretagne*—Brittany—and the northern coast of France. The Celtic traditions of his Breton heritage. The craggy cliffs and delicious *crêpes*. The family and friends he'd left behind.

For the past six years, he and Cardin—along with a regiment of four dozen royal knights from *le Château de Beaufort* in the northern Breton kingdom of Finistère—had defended the Atlantic coast of Aquitaine for King Philippe le Bel of France.

Sent by their own King Guillemin, a vassal of the French King Philippe, the Breton knights simultaneously squelched uprisings by English rebels anxious to claim the coveted duchy, while maintaining political alliances with the Spanish regions of Navarra and Aragón.

Far from their beloved Celtic home.

And for Cardin, far from horrific memories much too painful to confront.

The guards at the watchtower gate of *le Château de Montmarin* recognized the two brothers as fellow knights and allowed them entry through the outer curtain wall of the white limestone castle. Gaultier hauled Cardin across the inner bailey, through the enormous wooden entrance doors, and up the winding stone staircase to the third floor of the oceanfront fortress.

Along the length of the smooth stone walls, fragrant beeswax candles in metal sconces illuminated the dimly lit corridor. At the end of the long hall, Gaultier opened the heavy oak door which led into the modest quarters that the Breton brothers shared.

Inside their bedroom, two windows on the western wall opposite the entrance door offered a moonlit view of the tumultuous sea. On the left, embers banked in the stone fireplace emitted a gentle warmth against the damp evening chill. And along the right wall stood two beds, separated by a small table with an unlit candle and a pair of walnut chairs.

Gaultier seated a semiconscious Cardin on the edge

of the bed to remove his brother's blood-soaked clothing and ale-drenched leather boots. The repulsive, familiar stench of vomit and urine assailed his seasoned nostrils.

Mumbling incoherently in protest at being stripped of his filthy attire, a naked Cardin fell asleep almost instantly as soon as his injured head hit the straw-filled pillow.

Gaultier, eyeing the bruises, dried blood, and gruesome gash which a healer would need to treat tomorrow, tucked the woolen blankets over his sleeping brother's shoulder with an exasperated sigh of resignation. The gambling and drunken brawls were becoming increasingly frequent, extremely expensive, and exceedingly dangerous. Cardin was not only drowning his sorrow to escape his heart-wrenching past, but he was also acquiring far too many enemies, anxious for revenge.

This year, Gaultier vowed as he removed his own apparel and prepared for bed, he would bring Cardin home.

Even if he had to drag him—drunken, grumbling and unwilling—the entire length of France.

Chapter 2

A Wounded Heart

Amid the chirps and trills of morning larks and thrushes floating in upon the summer breeze, Laudine steeped the fragrant chamomile blossoms as she prepared a calming cup of *tisane*. From the cozy alcove of her castle kitchen, she gazed out the open window and watched the dark-haired Ulla—with her ever-present trained wolf at her side—gather yarrow, nettles, calendula, and red clover from the sheltered herb garden behind *le Château de Landuc*.

She'll prepare curative ointments and potions for our injured knights. If only an herbal elixir could heal her own wounded heart.

Ulla had first come to *le Château de Landuc* when she was twelve years old. Her parents, Viking descendants from Normandy, had sent their young daughter to study under the unparalleled tutelage of Laudine, the renowned Lady of the Sacred Spring and *châtelaine* of the famed medieval castle. As the highest ranking Priestess of Dana—Goddess of the Earth and embodiment of Mother Nature—Laudine practiced the traditional arts of Celtic healing, using the curative properties of the sacred elements of water, forest, and stone. Here in the Castle of Landuc, nestled in the dense

Forest of Brocéliande, Laudine taught young women to become *guérisseueses celtiques*, or capable Celtic healers.

And Ulla was undoubtedly the most gifted of them all.

While living in *le Château de Landuc*, studying herbal medicine in the Breton heart of the sacred forest, Ulla had been spared from the devastating illness that had claimed the lives of her entire family.

Laudine and her husband Esclados le Ros had subsequently sheltered Ulla in their castle, caring for her throughout adolescence, sharing the joy of her youthful exuberance, sublime singing voice, and extraordinary musical talent with the harp while watching her blossom into a beautiful young woman and exceptionally talented healer.

But tragically—for the second time in her young life—Ulla had returned home to Landuc.

To heal her grievously wounded heart.

"I've prepared us a pot of chamomile tea. Here, let me have those herbs while you join me in the alcove." Laudine took the straw basket from Ulla and set it upon the kitchen counter. She returned to the small nook where the dark-haired priestess with deep green eyes and a haunting smile sat at the rectangular oak table, the grey wolf Vill—the Norwegian word for fierce—lying protectively on the castle floor at Ulla's side.

Laudine poured and served two cups of *tisane*, placing the steaming teapot on the table between them as she settled into the walnut chair across from Ulla. She took a sip of the fragrant herbal tea, the slightly sweet flavor of honey lingering on her tongue as she hesitantly broached the delicate subject.

"My Yuletide wish is to have all three of my sons home for the holiday season." Laudine eyed Ulla over the rim of her ceramic cup, noting the younger woman's sorrowful smile and downturned gaze. "Bastien and his wife Gabrielle will be here, with their four children. And Lukaz, of course. He's six years old now…such a delightful little boy. It breaks my heart that his father— my wayward son Cardin—has never even seen his own child. The son he's scorned since birth." Laudine glanced out the window at the ripe wild plums on the abundant trees along the edge of the forest behind the castle, reminiscing about the shattered son she so desperately longed to see. *How he loved wild plum tarts as a little boy…* She smiled at the nostalgic memory, then returned her attention to Ulla. *"*For the past six years, I've begged him to come home for the Yuletide season, but he adamantly refuses to return to Bretagne. Cardin wants no part of his painful past. And that, dear Ulla, is why I need your assistance."

Ulla's inquisitive eyes—virid as the verdant forest—searched Laudine's face. Her dark brows lifted, forming the unspoken question. *How can I help?*

"I pray the Goddess will forgive me for the necessary lie, but I plan to feign a serious illness. With you as my healer, we'll convince everyone that I don't have much longer to live. I'll insist that my three sons come home to grant their mother's final request—to see them one last time before her impending demise." Laudine grinned conspiratorially at Ulla's astonished expression. "But you and I shall know the real reason for the ruse. To force Cardin home for the Yuletide holidays. And reunite father and son at long last."

Ulla's tragically beautiful face stretched into a

glorious smile. Dark green eyes sparkling like rare emeralds, the gifted healer sipped her chamomile tea and nodded in silent, eager agreement.

Like the fragile wings of a lark, hope fluttered softly in Laudine's loving heart.

Chapter 3

Basati

The salty brine of the ocean breeze and the squawk of seagulls roused Cardin de Landuc from a groggy, drunken sleep. He groaned as he tried to lift his throbbing head off the pillow. One of his eyes was swollen shut, so he could only peer at his surroundings from the corner of the other. He recognized the wooden table and two chairs against the stone wall. The empty bed near the exit door belonged to his older brother Gaultier. He was in his own bedroom in *le Château de Montmarin.*

Gaultier must have dragged him home from the tavern last night.

Again.

Like he'd done nearly every night since they'd come to Aquitaine six years ago.

A burning wound on his face reminded him of last night's drunken fight. He'd been gambling on dice, as usual, and had won several rounds of *passe-dix* when his opponent—an ornery shipping merchant named Andoni Zilar—had accused him of cheating and swung his fist into Cardin's jaw.

A few pirates and fishermen had joined in the fray, knocking down chairs and breaking glasses, when Zilar drew his jagged knife.

And—as an inebriated Cardin fought ineffectively to defend himself—carved a wicked gash in his left cheek.

Cardin couldn't remember anything after that. *I must have passed out on the table. Or been hit hard by one of Zilar's thugs.*

Cardin moaned as he rolled onto his back, his aching body battered and bruised. Dried blood adhered the pillow covering to the garish knife wound on his maimed face. His mouth was parched, and he desperately needed water.

And the chamber pot on the castle floor.

"*Egun on, mon frère.* It's about time you woke up." Gaultier spoke a *mélange* of the Basque dialect and their native French as he greeted his suffering, scarred brother. "I have a healer coming to treat your wounds. Here, drink this." He poured a large mug of watered ale from a pitcher and handed it to Cardin, who gulped it down greedily.

"I need to piss." A naked Cardin rose unsteadily to his feet and relieved himself in the chamber pot. When he'd finished, he scanned the room with his one good eye. "Where are my clothes?"

"They were covered in vomit, piss, and blood. I wanted to burn them, but the chambermaid insisted on washing them in the river. For now, you can wear these." Gaultier indicated a clean tunic and breeches lying on the adjacent bed. "*After* the healer treats you."

A knock at the door interrupted their conversation. At the entrance stood an older man with long grey hair and scraggly beard, holding a satchel of herbs. "*Egun on.* I'm Lasko, the healer you summoned."

With a wave of his hand, Gaultier beckoned the man

to enter. He indicated Cardin, sitting on the edge of the bed. "My brother was in a fight last night. At the Drunken Crow. A group of pirates attacked him, and one of them slashed his face. Can you stitch him up?"

Lasko grasped Cardin's jaw and tilted his patient's head toward the light coming in from the two windows overlooking the ocean. "Nasty wound. Good thing I've got herbs to prevent it from festering. *Bai,* I can stitch him up. But this will leave a jagged scar. Shame to ruin such a pretty face." The healer snickered gruffly, then flashed a wicked grin. "But some ladies *do* prefer a rugged look. Might be to your advantage after all."

Cardin scoffed as the healer applied a foul-smelling ointment to the burning slash on his left cheek. He didn't want to attract any ladies. He'd been actively avoiding them for the past six years.

Half an hour later, after Lasko had finished stitching up Cardin's wound, the healer gathered his salves and ointments, gratefully accepting the coin Gaultier offered him as payment. "*Eskerrak.* Thank you, Sir Gaultier." The old man addressed his bedridden patient while heading toward the exit door. "Take my advice. Stay away from Andoni Zilar and his henchmen. And avoid the Drunken Crow." A wary gleam in his wise eyes and a stern warning in his raspy voice, Lasko nodded farewell to the two brothers and retreated from the castle chamber.

"I'm off to the lists to train with the knights. You stay in bed and rest today. I'll bring food when I come back later." Gaultier donned his chain mail armor and coif headpiece, then strapped on his gleaming Spanish sword. His resolute expression and commanding tone brooked no argument. "Don't even think about going out tonight. I want an undisturbed evening with the beautiful Dolssa. You owe me that, little brother."

Cardin eased his bandaged, battered body down onto the bed, wincing in pain. "Agreed," he hissed between clenched teeth. "No taverns, gambling, or fighting. I give you my word." Cardin downed another mug of watered ale and set the empty container on the table between the two beds. "I'm in no condition to go anywhere." He gazed up at the dark-haired older brother who'd been like a guardian for the past six insufferable, desolate years. "Thanks for watching out for me."

"Someone has to, Basati. You don't care if you live or die. But *I do*." Gaultier grasped Cardin's shoulder and gave it an affectionate, fraternal squeeze. "Get some sleep. See you later."

As the heavy wooden door closed quietly behind Gaultier's retreating bulk, Cardin glanced at his sheathed dagger lying upon the bedside table.

An intricately carved head of a massive wolf adorned the elaborate hilt. The eye of the savage beast— a dark green faceted emerald—glinted in the morning light. Cardin reflected upon the weapon which had inspired his unique nickname. *Basati.* A Basque word for wolf, it also meant vicious brute. Barbarian.

Apt words to describe me.

Cardin placed a bent arm across his pounding forehead and sighed in exasperation, shame, and pain. He'd not always been a drunken rogue, gambling and dicing in local taverns and inns. He never used to brawl with pirates and marauders, sustaining grievous injuries and accruing powerful, vengeful enemies. He never used to drink himself senseless every night, seeking oblivion from the grief and guilt which gnawed mercilessly at his gut like the sharp, pointed fangs of a ravenous rodent.

Charlotte's ethereal face hovered above him.

Not since you were taken from me, my love.

Images of her were tantalizing. Taunting. Tormenting.

The long cascade of soft, golden curls. Brilliant eyes as blue as the Breton sea. Supple skin, soft as silk.

While his traitorous body throbbed with agonizing need, his broken heart clenched in shame.

Lust had caused his wife's death.

He, Cardin, had planted his seed deep in her fertile womb. And in doing so, had lost the woman who had meant more to him than life itself.

He could still hear her heart-wrenching screams. Three torturous days of unbearable agony as she struggled to give birth. And finally, on the Winter Solstice—the darkest day of the year when night overwhelms the light—his beloved wife sacrificed her life to bring forth his heir.

The infant Cardin had rejected since birth.

The son he had never even seen.

Lukaz.

When the midwife—her arms still dripping with Charlotte's lifeblood—had offered the squalling babe for Cardin to hold, he'd refused. Instead, he'd gathered his beloved wife in shaking arms, bellowed like a wounded beast, and retreated, numb with shock, to his isolated private chamber.

His sister-in-law Gabrielle had assured Cardin the wet nurse would feed and care for the motherless, hungry babe. An indifferent Cardin made no effort to see his newborn son.

After the funeral, Cardin returned Charlotte's

dowry—including the demesne and manor house in Saint-Renan where they had lived and she had died—to her grateful, grieving parents.

His older brother Bastien had insisted that Cardin and his infant son Lukaz come live with his wife Gabrielle and him at *le Château de Beaufort*, where Cardin and his two older siblings had trained and now served as royal knights to Gabrielle's father, King Guillemin of Finistère.

And Cardin, a ghostlike guest in the castle for three endless, empty months, kept to his solitary room.

And refused to see his infant son.

Servants brought him food, which he left largely untouched.

Bastien and Gaultier tried to coax him back to the lists to train with the Breton knights of Beaufort.

But it was Gabrielle's royal father, King Guillemin of Finistère—loyal vassal to King Philippe le Bel of France—who had offered the solution to Cardin's intolerable suffering.

The chance to flee from debilitating pain.

The opportunity to escape the constant reminders of the joyous life he had lost.

By venturing to distant Aquitaine, the vast province along the Atlantic coastline of southwestern France near the border with Spain.

Accompanied by his older brother Gaultier and four dozen Breton knights from Finistère, Cardin would reside in Biarritz, the heart of the Basque country, in the clifftop castle of *le Château de Montmarin.* To defend King Philippe's precarious hold on the valuable duchy of Aquitaine against the English rebels who claimed it as theirs.

And so, for the past six interminable years, Cardin—nicknamed Basati for the wolf-head knife that he wielded and the vicious brute he'd become—had defended the French King Philippe of Paris.

Obeyed his sovereign lord, King Guillemin of Finistère.

And tried, unsuccessfully, to drown his guilt and grief in causing his wife's death and abandoning his infant son.

In every raucous, riotous tavern in town.

Chapter 4

Solace in Silence

Ulla headed toward her small stone cottage with the thatched roof in the thick woods beyond the castle grounds. Her wolf Vill was anxious to hunt—as the two of them usually did every morning, with Ulla's peregrine falcon, Finn. But first, she needed to store the herbs that she'd gathered in her workshop. And prepare the salves, ointments, and tinctures she needed to treat her patients and any villagers who fell ill.

Since Ulla was mute, she summoned Vill with a distinctive whistle and commanded him with hand gestures. When she'd found him three years ago as a critically injured pup, his right rear leg had been impossibly ensnared in a rabbit trap. He'd been close to death—frightened, bloody, and starving—but Ulla had managed to cut the metal snare and free the young wolf. She'd carried him home and applied soothing comfrey and yarrow to stanch the bleeding and prevent the wound in his leg from festering. She'd fed him raw eggs, scraps of meat, and sheep's milk until he'd regained his strength. Slowly and patiently, she'd trained him to come when she whistled, to stay with an outstretched palm, and to hunt cooperatively with Finn.

Born the daughter of a Viking chieftain, Ulla was

permitted to own a peregrine falcon, a privilege reserved for nobility. During her adolescence at *le Château de Landuc,* while studying to become a Celtic healer, Ulla had worked alongside the castle falconer, training Finn with jesses, bells, and hoods, until the bird was able to perch on her wrist and hunt game with swift, lethal precision.

Once Vill had learned to obey her whistle and hand commands, Ulla trained him to hunt at her side with Finn. Her falcon would attack birds in the sky or small animals on land—such as rabbits or squirrels—and her wolf would retrieve the prey for the three of them to share.

Although Finn lived in the castle mews with the other falcons and hawks, Ulla fetched her each day to hunt with Vill in the dense Forest of Brocéliande. She would head over there as soon as she finished preparing her salves and tinctures.

Ulla entered the grey stone cottage where she lived alone with Vill, setting the basket of herbs on her kitchen counter and closing the solid oak door behind them. In the hearth on the left wall, banked embers glowed, emitting a soft warmth to counter the early morning chill. *I'll stoke the fire after we return from the hunt. Hopefully, we'll have rabbit for a stew. Or perhaps thrush, lark, or partridge. It depends on what prey Finn will hunt.*

She glanced out the kitchen window to the tree-enclosed back yard where her three hens poked at insects in the grassy meadow. She'd taught Vill to leave them alone, for Ulla depended on their eggs for the *omelettes aux champignons* she often prepared with mushrooms and fresh herbs.

Opening the rear door of the kitchen, Ulla stepped down the stone stairs, with Vill close behind. She went inside the henhouse and gathered the three fresh eggs. *I'll use these for my supper tonight. And give Vill a large helping of raw meat from the hunt.*

After she'd collected the eggs, Ulla harvested a few carrots and potatoes from her small vegetable garden to add with fresh herbs to the stew. Satisfied that she had what was needed for today's meals, she whistled for Vill and went back into the cottage to prepare her herbal treatments.

In a small alcove off the kitchen, Ulla hung a few herbs to dry from hooks in the wooden ceiling. On the countertop, she separately ground sage, garlic, willow bark, comfrey, and red clover, storing each in distinct, stoppered jars. She steeped tinctures to strain later when she returned from the hunt, and prepared elixirs from ginger, red clover, and burdock root, which she placed in small glass vials. As she wrote the names of the herbs on affixed labels, she reflected how fortunate she was to be able to read and write, for many of the villagers— especially women—could not. But Laudine, the Lady of *le Château de Landuc*, insisted that all of her priestesses learn to read and write as an integral part of their instruction as Celtic healers.

Vill, lying on the floor near her feet, his large head resting on his enormous front paws, whimpered his plea to go hunting.

I sometimes wish I could speak to him, as I once did with Finn. But trauma stole my voice three years ago. And I have found solace in silence ever since.

With a hand gesture, she ordered her impatient companion to stay just a bit longer while she worked.

Once she'd finished preparing the ointments, elixirs, and tonics, Ulla put away her mortar and pestle, stored the herbal supplies, and tidied her workshop.

Vill's amber eyes followed her every movc.

Ulla strapped the dagger at her ankle, the bow and quiver of arrows on her back, and the leather falconry glove on her left hand. When she finally whistled, the grey wolf lurched to his feet, shaking his bristled fur in eager anticipation of the hunt. Close on her heels, he followed Ulla out the front door of the cottage. Bounding past her, he ran and spun in exuberant circles, leaping into the air with the thrill of unbridled joy.

Ulla laughed silently, her suffering spirit soaring free.

Together, they romped across the meadow toward the castle stables, where Quentin, the Master of Horse at *le Château de Landuc*, greeted Ulla and her wolf with a hearty grin. "I'll have Argant saddle her for you, Lady Ulla. Nåde is as anxious for the hunt as Vill." Tossing his long, sandy hair over a lanky shoulder, Quentin summoned the stable boy with a jut of his bearded chin.

A few moments later, the magnificent black Friesian nickered in greeting when the lad led Nåde—the Norwegian word for grace—toward Ulla. He handed her the reins and helped her climb up into the saddle.

Ulla smiled and nodded her head in gratitude. With a wave goodbye and a whistle for Vill, she rode off toward the castle mews to fetch her falcon Finn.

****

The crisp green scent of pine mingled with the earthy aroma of rich loam and decaying leaves as Ulla galloped through the lush forest with Vill at her side. Flying high above the beech, fir, and oak trees—well beyond the reach of Ulla's arrows— Finn hunted as the summer sun dappled through the dense Forest of Brocéliande.

The wind whipped her long black hair, her spirit soaring freely with Finn, as Nåde galloped and Vill raced across the forested ground.

Ulla much preferred the silent company of animals over the garrulous presence of people who made the loss of her speaking voice a painful reminder of the horrific past. Once, she'd sung like a lark, her melodic voice in perfect harmony with the mellow notes of the golden harp her fingers had so lovingly strummed. She'd often regaled the entire *Château de Landuc* with sublime music, her soul unleashed like Finn now winging through the cerulean sky. But shock stole her speech and silenced her song, rendering Ulla as mute as the trees.

A shrill screech announced Finn's predatory plummet as she dove from the sky and seized a rabbit with her sharp, extended talons. Vill raced ahead to retrieve the game while Ulla reined her mare and dismounted. The wolf returned a few moments later, dropping the prey from his shaggy maw onto the leaves at Ulla's booted feet.

She bent down and scooped up the rabbit, securing it with the others strapped to Nåde's saddle. *I'll cure and dry these skins. And use the fur to line a winter cloak. The perfect Yuletide gift for Laudine.*

Satisfied with the quantity of game obtained from the hunt, Ulla mounted her horse and whistled for Finn to return and perch upon her gloved wrist. With a different whistle reserved for Vill, she summoned her wolf and rode back through the forest toward the castle mews.

Ulla returned her bird to the falconer, dismounted her glossy black Friesian, and motioned for Vill to stay at Nåde's side. Retrieving one of the rabbits strapped to the horse's saddle, she followed the falconer Gauvin into the mews where several other hawks and hunting birds roosted at different levels within the large, domed wooden building. While Gauvin set Finn upon her reserved perch, Ulla unsheathed her dagger and cut pieces of raw meat, which she fed to her ravenous raptor.

Once Finn had eaten her fill, Ulla caressed the falcon's head as she prepared to depart.

Gauvin tucked a strand of grey hair behind his ear and smiled at Ulla. "*À demain, Madame*. See you tomorrow."

Ulla smiled softly, ducked her chin in gratitude, and returned to her awaiting horse and wolf. She climbed back into the saddle, galloped across the castle grounds to the stables, and dismounted, stroking her horse's muzzle as she handed the reins to a grinning Quentin.

He takes such good care of Nåde. I've prepared a skin ointment for his wife Rozenn. She'll appreciate it as her stomach stretches during these last few weeks of her breeding. At the thought of the impending birth, Ulla's throat clenched. Laudine would be the midwife to deliver the baby. Ulla could not bear to be around infants, nursing mothers, or small children. The pain still sliced like a knife.

She retrieved the salve from the sack strapped to Nåde's saddle, placing the small jar inside Quentin's palm and closing his fingers around it. As she gazed up into his inquisitive eyes, she smiled softly to convey her thankfulness. With hand gestures, she indicated that the balm was intended to soothe the stretching skin for

Rozenn's enormous stomach.

"Thank you very much, Lady Ulla. My wife will be most grateful, for her skin is indeed very itchy." He tucked the jar into the pocket of his breeches and turned as the stable boy approached to fetch Nåde. "Argant here will take excellent care of your Friesian. He'll water her, wash her down. Curry her coat and mane. Feed her a bucket of fresh oats, too. He mucked out the stall while you were hunting. He's a good lad." Quentin handed the reins to the bashful young groom, who promptly led the horse across the grassy field toward the stables where Lord Esclados—Laudine's husband and *châtelain* of Castle Landuc—kept and bred his magnificent horses.

Quentin kissed Ulla's hand. "Thank you again. We're most grateful to have such a capable healer. See you tomorrow, my lady. *À demain.*" Kind eyes sparkling in the late morning sun, the Master of Horse of *le Château de Landuc* smiled as he waved goodbye and strode away.

Ulla whistled for Vill and returned with her wolf to the grey stone cottage nestled in the dense Breton woods.

Inside her home, she strode into the cozy wooden kitchen and laid the fresh game upon the counter. She peeked out the open window and spotted the hens grazing in the back meadow among the pink, mauve, and heather blossoms enclosed by abundant oaks, beech, and fruit-laden trees.

I'll pick some plums and make a tarte aux mirabelles to bring when I visit Laudine tomorrow. She and Lord Esclados both love my wild plum tarts. Chuckling silently, Ulla returned to the open living room area and stoked the fire in the hearth where she would soon simmer a savory rabbit stew with fresh herbs from the castle garden.

But first, from the hungry look in his watchful amber eyes, Vill needed to eat several pounds of raw meat. As a skilled hunter and reliable retriever, he deserved a just reward.

Unsheathing the dagger from her ankle, Ulla scraped the meat and bones from the carcasses of eight rabbits, carefully preserving the skins to clean and cure for Laudine's Yuletide cloak. Setting aside the meat from one rabbit which she would use in the stew, Ulla placed the remainder of the fresh game in Vill's large wooden bowl.

At her whistle, the ravenous wolf pounced greedily on his much-anticipated meal.

While Vill noisily devoured the delicious contents in his dish, Ulla cut the remaining meat into small pieces and added it to a pot of water, pouring in a cup of red wine for full-bodied flavor and a dollop of lard as a tenderizer. She peeled and sliced carrots, potatoes, garlic, onions, and mushrooms, placing the vegetables into the cauldron. For a final touch, she chopped fresh thyme, marjoram, rosemary, and sage, sprinkling the savory herbs over the contents of the stew.

She covered the pot, set it over the hearth, and turned to see that Vill had finished eating. From the bucket she'd pumped that morning at the well, she poured fresh water into a clean bowl for Vill to drink. He slurped and sloshed it all over the wooden floor.

With another silent chuckle, Ulla wiped up the spill with a drying cloth. Then, grabbing her satchel of herbs, she whistled for Vill and left the cottage, headed across the verdant forest to check in on her recovering patient.

****

"He's doing much better, thanks to those drops you put in his ear. Now the pain and fever are both gone." The young mother, Enora, swept a lock of brown hair from the sleeping face of her bedridden three-year-old son.

Ulla's palms became damp, her mouth went dry, and her heart began to race.

"And the calendula ointment quickly healed the wound on my husband's arm. We are most grateful for your service, Ulla. Please accept these pelts as payment. I know you make lovely cloaks, hats, and gloves with the fur." Her relieved, maternal face illuminated with a thankful smile, Enora offered Ulla an assortment of pelts in her outstretched arms.

Ulla bowed her head to convey gratitude as she accepted approximately two dozen hides of rabbit, squirrel, muskrat, and beaver. *These will be perfect for lining gloves and trimming cloaks for Yuletide gifts. I'll sew one for Quentin's wife. And their new baby.*

Unbidden images of bright blue eyes and soft brown curls floated into her mind, robbing Ulla of breath and thought. She quickly ducked her chin to hide her distress, securing the pelts into the satchel slung across her shoulder. Inhaling deeply to calm her ragged nerves, she straightened her back, shook Enora's grateful hand with a masked smile, and escaped outside to whistle for Vill.

Tears streaming down her cheeks, she plodded blindly through the dense forest, her loyal wolf at her side, desperate for the sanctity of her silent stone cottage. Pulse pounding furiously, limbs shaky and weak, she opened the front door and followed Vill inside the solid structure. She locked the door behind her and collapsed against the hard wood for support as she struggled to catch her breath.

Every time I even think of a babe, I can't breathe. I already avoid Lysara, because I can't bear to be near her infant son. What will I do when everyone comes to the castle for the Yuletide season? Rozenn's babe will be born by then. And Nolwenn's, too. Laudine wants her three sons and their young children home for the holidays. How will I cope with so many adorable babies and cuddly little ones who remind me of my own tragic loss? Please, dear Goddess, give me strength. I cannot endure any more.

Ulla slid to the floor and buried her face in the hands resting on her bent knees. And—as Vill frantically licked her cheeks with his long, loving pink tongue—wept for her lost baby boy.

Chapter 5

The Head of the Wolf

Andoni Zilar gazed at the turbulent ocean from the open window of the two-story building where he conducted a flourishing shipping business in the seaside village of Biarritz. He inhaled the briny breeze, methodically contemplating the intricate details of his ingenious plan.

Last night, he'd won fifty pounds of silver from the Basque Beast, Basati. Zilar had flagrantly cheated, knowing that Basati would realize he'd used a pair of altered dice. As expected, there'd been a scuffle, which had led to a brawl. And he' d carved a jagged gash in Basati's scowling lupine face.

Zilar had deliberately baited the hungry, angry wolf.

And tonight, he'd lure Basati into the awaiting trap.

Zilar had come up with the ideal means of eliminating the troublesome Comte Eztebe Ibarra, Lord of *le Château de Montmarin.*

A staunch supporter of both King Guillemin of Finistère and King Philippe of France, Ibarra opposed the English claims to Aquitaine and therefore stood in the way of Zilar's profitable trade with King Edward Longshanks. Ibarra would soon depart for Paris, to formalize the Alliance with Aquitaine treaty which would give the Iron King Philippe control of all shipping from Aquitaine to England. As King of Navarra as well as France, Philippe le Bel would thus control the entire Atlantic seaboard from the northwest shores of Spain to the distant coast of Bretagne, all the way to the mouth of the Seine River flowing into Paris.

By removing Ibarra—the painful thorn in Longshanks' side and crucial component of the Alliance with Aquitaine—Zilar would be handsomely rewarded by the powerful English monarch. King Edward Longshanks was also the Duke of Aquitaine. And—as an incentive for preventing the disastrous alliance with King Philippe of France—he'd promised to appoint Zilar as lord of the magnificent oceanfront castle.

Le Château de Montmarin.

From his superior stronghold on the strategic cliff of Biarritz, Zilar would then have complete command of trade in the Basque region of France as Aquitaine's royal shipping merchant to England. He'd vastly increase his wealth with exclusive rights to transport expensive Bordeaux wines and other luxury goods to the affluent English king. With the financial support of the Spanish King of Aragón—an ally of Longshanks as well as the titled Count of Provence and Lord of Montpellier—Zilar would gain access to the lucrative shipping industry along the entire French Mediterranean coast.

Indeed, by eliminating Comte Eztebe Ibarra, Zilar would ensure his financial future as the most powerful and wealthy shipping merchant in all of France.

And the Basque wolf Basati would be blamed for the crime.

Zilar had selected Sir Cardin de Landuc—whose Basque nickname was Basati—after carefully researching his dubious past.

De Landuc was one of four dozen Breton knights sent by King Guillemin of Finistère—loyal vassal of the French king, Philippe le Bel—to the oceanfront castle of Montmarin.

For the past six years, Cardin de Landuc—Basati— and the royal French guards had squelched English uprisings in southwestern France, thereby solidifying King Philippe's claims to the territory of Aquitaine, while simultaneously defending the oceanfront fortress of Comte Ibarra, staunch ally of the Iron King Philippe.

Zilar chuckled at his ingenious plan.

With Basati's well-known weakness for wagering on dice and his staggering debt to the Basque Lord Itzal Baroja, he was the perfect victim.

Tonight, Basati would fall into the trap.

And Zilar would ensnare the Basque wolf from Bretagne.

****

Cardin stretched his arms overhead, wincing at the pain in his ribs. He sat idly on the side of his bed, staring out the open window, watching the ocean waves crash on the cliff far below the castle.

As promised, his brother Gaultier had sent a steaming platter of fresh seafood from the castle kitchen.

Cardin had eaten his fill of scallops, shrimp, and oysters.

He'd taken a long afternoon nap.

And now, he was restless, cranky, and bored.

He'd sworn to Gaultier that he would stay home tonight. That he would not drink ale or mead. He'd refrain from dicing. And above all, he would avoid the irresistible lure of the iniquitous Drunken Crow.

As Cardin reminded himself for the hundredth time that he would not leave the castle and would uphold his oath to his older brother, Xabi burst into the room, breathless with excitement.

"Basati—you have to come with me! Andoni Zilar is hosting a game of Hazard tonight at the Drunken Crow. But he'll only play against *you*." Xabi's eagle eyes gleamed in the golden light of the setting sun. "Zilar has challenged you to wager one hundred pounds of silver. He's giving you the chance to *double* what you lost last night! You can pay off your debt to Baroja. And—with side bets—I can win enough to buy Euri a wedding ring. *Goazen,* Basati. C'mon, let's go!"

Cardin contemplated the wildly exuberant, heavily bearded face of his best friend. One of the intrepid knights of *le Château de Montmarin* who defended his sovereign lord Eztebe Ibarra, Xabi loved drinking and dicing as much as tilting in the lists.

Just like Cardin himself.

Remembering his vow to Gaultier, Cardin reluctantly lowered his eyes and shamefully shook his head. "I can't. I promised to stay home tonight. No wagering. No ale. No drunken brawls in local taverns. Gaultier deserves an uninterrupted night with Dolssa. I owe him that."

"You can get revenge on Zilar for carving up your face. Take all his bloody silver. Humiliate him in front of all his men. And win enough to get Baroja off your back." Xabi's lips curled up in a smug smirk. "Tonight— in honor of the high stakes in the game—the Drunken Crow is serving *golden mead*."

Cardin's mouth went dry and his palms became damp. He loved golden mead. Almost as much as dicing.

And Hazard was the most thrilling game of all.

He could examine Zilar's dice. There'd be no chance for him to cheat again.

I'll win back the silver I lost last night. Settle my debt with Baroja. Give Xabi the chance to buy a wedding ring for Euri.

And get back to the castle before Gaultier returns.

Cardin's bandaged, bloodied face broke into a wicked, wolfish grin. "I never could resist golden mead."

****

The raucous revelry inside the noisy tavern was music to Cardin's edgy ears.

In the rear of the cavernous room, beyond the mahogany bar which lined the right wall, lively tunes floated from fiddles, flutes and rebecs. Jubilant customers chatted boisterously at crowded tables, feasting on aromatic seafood as coquettish tavern wenches served abundant mugs of golden mead.

In the center of the inn, four tables had been placed together and covered with a white tablecloth, forming a long rectangular area for dicing. Eager participants were lined up on either side, silver coins clutched in their impatient hands, greedy grins upon their avid, anxious faces.

At the far end of the gaming table stood Andoni Zilar, a snide smirk upon his scarred, sneering visage. Tall and lanky, with dark eyes and greasy black hair that reached his broad shoulders, the wealthy shipping merchant with a penchant for gambling twirled his narrow mustache and snickered as Cardin strode up to the table. "Come to lose more silver, Basati? I'll be happy to take your hundred pounds. Because that's the wager. Do you accept the challenge? Or are your bollocks not big enough?"

Snickers and jeers floated around the table as Cardin held Zilar's taunting stare. "I accept the challenge. Place your wager. But before you roll, I want to inspect the dice. Can't have you cheating. *Like last night*." Although it stretched and pulled the stitches in his mutilated face, Cardin ignored the burning pain as he grinned, holding out his calloused palm.

A collective hush swept across the suddenly silent room when the musicians abruptly stopped playing. Patrons of the inn quickly gathered around to watch as Zilar and Basati— the two most competitive gamblers in all of Biarritz—provided the evening's exciting entertainment.

Zilar scoffed and tossed the dice to Cardin, who made a theatrical display of examining them before returning the ivory-colored bone cubes for the initial roll.

"Seven is the main." Twirling his thin, dark mustache, Zilar gloated over the good fortune of his first throw. Seven gave him the best odds of *nicking* as the caster in the complicated rules of Hazard.

While the two adversaries glowered at each other with seething animosity and venomous rivalry, side wagers were quickly placed against Zilar's next throw.

Cheers and shouts from the wildly exuberant audience reverberated across the tavern when Zilar rolled a two, thereby losing the round.

A grinning Cardin collected twenty pounds of his slimy opponent's silver.

Dark eyes gleaming with glee, Xabi greedily scooped up the coins from his winning side bet and slid them into the black velvet pouch belted at his waist.

Zilar threw the dice again, winning the next round

with a main of six and a nick of twelve. But when he lost the next two consecutive rolls, it was Cardin's turn as caster.

Eyeing the cocky opponent who toyed with the dark hair above his sneering lip, Cardin took a long pull of mead, savoring the sweet honey flavor as much as the thrill of winning Zilar's silver. He'd won sixty pounds so far, and with luck would win forty more. Enough to clear his stifling debt with Baroja. And get the notorious Basque moneylender off his back.

Cardin cast the dice, rolling a five for the main, and side bets were placed on whether he would nick, out, or chance. He rolled another five to nick the round and win another twenty pounds.

Xabi guffawed with gusty approval, sliding more silver coins into his black velvet pouch.

As he guzzled his goblet of mead, Cardin considered his good fortune.

He'd easily won eighty pounds of Zilar's silver.

Too easily.

Something wasn't right.

But while doubt niggled at the back of his mind, the lure of the game was irresistible.

Cardin cupped the dice in his fists. Raised them to his lips. And blew on them for luck. Rattling the ivory cubes by rubbing them loudly between his palms, he hurled the dice onto the table, rolling an eight for the main.

And nicked with a twelve for the win.

Xabi leapt into the air, hooting and hollering with joy.

Several of the Breton knights who had won side bets gripped Cardin's shoulder with gratitude and vigorously shook his hand. The jovial innkeeper—thankful that Cardin had not caused a destructive brawl and had instead attracted a thirsty crowd—heartily congratulated him on the win and rewarded him with a pitcher of golden mead.

A scowling Zilar—closely followed by his dozen loyal henchmen and a few disgruntled losers—stormed from the inn, muttering expletives and cursing Cardin's incredible luck.

Musicians resumed their lively play. Patrons began to dance. And Cardin, securing his silver in two sturdy bags to carry back to the castle, exited the noisy inn with Xabi.

"You took all his silver. Got your revenge. And now, you can settle your debt with Baroja. And I'll buy the wedding ring for Euri. God's bones, Basati! You won a bloody hundred pounds!" Xabi's white teeth gleamed in the moonlight as the two men strode up the cobblestoned path toward the towering *Château de Montmarin* at the top of the oceanfront cliff.

The hairs on the back of Cardin's neck stiffened in sudden warning. But, hindered by the weight of the bags of silver, he was unable to draw his dagger as a dozen henchmen emerged from the shadows.

With a sickening thud, the back of his head exploded in blinding, debilitating pain.

And Cardin succumbed into darkness.

****

Andoni Zilar sat at his oval table, savoring the rich Basque wine, patiently awaiting the return of his reliable, impeccable men.

The closing and latching sounds of the heavy front door announced their arrival.

"We seized the silver, my lord." The coins clinked and jingled as Urdin—his bearded face partially concealed by the dark woolen cloak—hoisted the two heavy bags onto the wooden table.

Zilar eyed the black velvet sacks, caring little for the contents. The staged theft of the silver masked the real reason for the robbery. Pulse pounding in his parched, tight throat, he leaned forward in breathless anticipation. "And the knife?"

"*Hemen, nagusi.* Here it is, boss." Gizon—Zilar's most skilled thief—proudly laid the prized dagger before his exigent, exacting lord.

Zilar tilted the treasured weapon in his hand, admiring the exquisite details in the glowing candlelight.

The sleek, sharp, lethal blade.

The curved bone handle with the glittering emerald eye.

And—carved into the hilt—the distinctive feature that every citizen in Biarritz would recognize.

The damning evidence which would implicate Basati in Ibarra's assassination.

The massive head of a snarling, savage wolf.

Chapter 6

Back to Brocéliande

Gaultier loved her luxurious chestnut hair. Her dark brown eyes, smoldering with desire. Her soft, smooth skin, seductively scented with rosewater. The voluptuous curves that drove him absolutely wild.

Cradled in his sinewy arms, a long, lean leg draped across his hip, she was a tantalizing temptress. And he could never get enough.

He—the wandering knight who'd always flitted from females like a bee collecting nectar from flowers—had finally fallen.

And fallen hard.

For the bewitching Basque beauty.

Dolssa.

Tonight—at long last—she was his.

He swooped down again to taste her full, luscious lips. Roamed his eager, appreciative hands over her tiny waist and rounded hips.

He'd already made mad, passionate love to her.

Twice.

But, by the Goddess, he wanted her again.

Gaultier devoured her lush mouth, parting her sensuous lips with a probing, penetrating tongue. As his hardening shaft awakened for the third exquisite plunge into Dolssa's delicious depths, a thunderous pounding on the wooden door jolted Gaultier to his feet. Lunging for the sword which leaned against the wooden wall, he unsheathed his blade and bellowed at the unwelcome intrusion. "Who goes there?"

A frantic male voice replied, "Sir Gaultier! There's been an attack. It's your brother Basati. Come quickly, my lord!"

Gaultier cursed with an equal measure of frustration and fury.

He gazed longingly at the frightened Dolssa, sitting upright in her rumpled bed, clutching the bedsheets to cover the luscious breasts he desperately longed to caress with ardent lips, fingers, and tongue.

He'd finally made love to her—claimed her as his own—after months of patient, persistent courtship. A tavern maid at the Sultry Siren where he'd frequently bedded many a willing wench, he'd met Dolssa this past spring when she began serving customers at the inn. At first, he'd thought she was like the other ladies— available to satisfy sailors, pirates, and lusty knights like himself. But he'd soon learned that she was a mere server of seafood and mead.

And definitely not for sale.

So, he'd wooed her. Pined for her. And—little by little as he'd slowly and gradually won her pure, generous heart—had lost his own to the inimitable, intriguing Basque beauty.

Dolssa.

Tonight, in making to love to her, he'd glimpsed heaven. Physical bliss and merging of souls, unlike anything he'd ever experienced before. He'd lost himself in her. And he wanted so very much more.

But Cardin, the bloody bastard, had done it again. Ruined a perfect evening with Dolssa.

Despite his solemn vow to stay confined to the castle.

Abrupt, insistent pummeling interrupted Gaultier's train of thoughts. "Sir Gaultier! *S'il vous plaît, Monsieur.* Open the door!"

Gaultier apologized to Dolssa as he quickly donned his breeches and tunic, strapped on his belt, and sheathed his sword. "I'm sorry, *ma mignonne.* It seems my brother has started another brawl." He plopped down on the bed, pulled her into his arms, and kissed her softly. Brushing a silky lock of dark tresses from her thick lashes, he gently stroked her flushed cheek. "I'll drag him back to the castle. Post guards at the chamber door. And make it up to you tomorrow night." He lifted her slender hand and brushed his lips upon her long fingers. "I promise."

He stood and pulled the surcoat over his chainmail armor. With one last look of longing, he bade farewell to Dolssa.

And strode across the room to open the oaken door.

Two of his fellow Breton knights anxiously awaited in the long wooden hall dimly lit by tallow candles in metal wall sconces. Blond head bowed humbly before his higher-ranking lord, Guenole stammered, "Sorry to disturb you, sir. But your brother and Xabi have been robbed and beaten. They're lying in a dark alley behind the Drunken Crow."

"Take me to them." Gaultier donned his coif and followed the two knights down the hall. They swiftly descended the stairs, crossed the animated tavern, and exited the Sultry Siren into the salty air of the starry night sky.

When they arrived at the scene of the assault, half a dozen knights stood guard around Cardin and Xabi, who were battered and bloody, lying face down on the cobblestoned street. Lasko the healer was bent over the victims' bodies, tending to their injuries.

Gaultier rushed to his brother's side and knelt beside the grey-haired, elderly man.

"There's a large, egg-shaped swelling on the back of his head." Lasko pointed to the wound which indicated how Cardin had been ambushed. "Dried blood and matted hair, but I see no other damage. Same for that knight over there." He referred to Xabi with a jut of his bearded chin. "I've cleansed their wounds, but there's no need for bandages. They might be a bit groggy when they wake up. But both will be fine tomorrow."

Gaultier thanked the healer, paid him with coin, and ordered two knights to escort the old man safely home. As he watched the trio depart, one of his guards approached to render a report.

"Basati won at dice tonight, my lord." Koneg—one of Gaultier's Breton knights from the kingdom of Finistère—informed him of the evening's events. "Andoni Zilar challenged him to a game of Hazard. Your brother won a hundred pounds of silver. Xabi won twenty pounds through side bets as well. The two of them left the tavern and were on their way back to the castle when they were attacked and robbed. All the silver is gone, sir."

Dicing, drinking, and debts. They'll be the death of him yet. Gaultier nodded gratefully to Koneg in acknowledgment. He returned to his prone brother, who had begun to stir with a low, grumbling groan.

"Let's get them back to the castle." Gaultier turned

toward two of his Breton knights standing near the victims. "Guenole, you and Yann take Xabi to his room. Get him settled. I'll see you tomorrow in the lists. *Trugarez. Noz vat.* Thank you and good night."

While his men carried Xabi up the cobblestone path to *le Château de Montmarin* at the top of the hill, Gaultier knelt beside Cardin and slid his arms under his brother's broad shoulders. With Koneg lifting Cardin's feet, the two of them hauled the bulky brute home.

****

"You bastard. You *promised* me that you'd stay in the castle. That I wouldn't have to come peel your bloody ass off some vomit-strewn table in a tavern. Lugh's balls, Basati! I was in Dolssa's bed!" Spittle flew as an enraged Gaultier struggled to control his fury while removing Cardin's blood-soaked tunic.

"*Désolé, mon frère.* I'm sorry." Cardin hung his head in shame. "I needed the silver to pay Baroja. And I won a hundred pounds tonight. Enough to clear my debt. But Xabi and I were robbed behind the Drunken Crow."

With Gaultier's help, Cardin removed his boots, then rose unsteadily to unbuckle his leather belt.

The sheath was empty. Frantic, he patted the waistband of his breeches, searching for the missing knife. "Bastards stole my dagger, too. The one with the head of the wolf."

Gaultier took the leather belt with the empty sheath from him and laid it on the wooden table beside the bed. "You can borrow one of mine." He swung Cardin's legs up on the bed and gently eased his injured head back onto the pillow. "The healer said you'd need to rest for a day or two. So you're staying in bed. And I'm posting guards outside the door to make sure you do."

Pulling himself up to his full, towering height, Gaultier smoothed his long dark hair and straightened the surcoat which covered his chainmail armor.

In the incandescent light from the candle on the bedside table, Cardin gazed at the five ermine symbols over the black lion and golden-horned ram. The royal coat of arms of King Guillemin and the Breton kingdom of Finistère which he and Gaultier loyally served.

Le Château de Beaufort.

La Bretagne.

Home.

Cardin clamped his eyes shut, his throat constricting in a smothering wave of guilt and grief.

Charlotte. I miss you so much I can't breathe.

Lukaz. The son I abandoned at birth.

I'm a royal knight of Beaufort. Yet I live in disgrace, dishonor, and despair.

Lugh's balls, I need a mug of mead!

Gaultier's deep baritone permeated Cardin's pain. "Two days for you to heal. For our knights to load the horses and supplies. Now that we've achieved our king's goals, and the Alliance with Aquitaine is secure, you and I are leaving Biarritz, little brother."

Having removed his armor, Gaultier sighed as he plopped down on the bed to pull off his heavy boots. "*Maman* is gravely ill. She's called us home. Her Yuletide wish is to have us there at her side. And so, *mon frère*—you can't refuse this time. Even if I have to drag you, kicking and screaming, the entire length of France—we're returning to Bretagne. You and I are going back to Brocéliande."

Chapter 7

A Wounded Little Wolf

Laudine removed the stems from the dried rosemary, sage, calendula, and yarrow for Ulla to grind with a mortar and pestle as the two priestesses prepared herbal remedies in the corner of the castle kitchen of *le Château de Landuc*. "Thank you for writing the letter to Gaultier as my healer. Although I hate to deceive my sons, feigning a grave illness was the only way I could think of to convince Cardin to come home. The letter you sent should have arrived in Aquitaine by now. But it will take at least six to eight weeks for Gaultier and Cardin to travel home from *le Château de Montmarin* in Biarritz. I'm hoping they'll arrive in late August. I'll keep them here throughout the Yuletide season. And try to reunite father and son."

Ulla smiled and nodded, mixing the ground yarrow into beeswax to create a curative salve for wounds.

"Bastien and Gabrielle have taken excellent care of Lukaz these past six years since Cardin abandoned him and left for Biarritz. Lukaz has lived with his aunt and uncle since birth—they've been the boy's parents, raising him like their own son. Lukaz' maternal grandparents passed away shortly after his mother Charlotte's death. He doesn't understand why his Papa never comes home to visit and never writes any letters, like the fathers of the other young squires do at *le Château de Beaufort.*" Laudine poured steaming water over elderberry leaves, steeping them in a bowl to prepare an herbal elixir.

"Gabrielle and Bastien have told Lukaz that his Papa—the noble Sir Cardin de Landuc—is the finest archer among the royal knights sent by King Guillemin to defend the valuable province of Aquitaine. Lukaz knows that his Papa's nickname is Basati—the Basque Wolf—and he's proud that Gabrielle calls him Little Wolf, after his father. He even wants to become a castle archer, just like his Papa. That's why Esclados and I are giving him a new bow and quiver of arrows when he arrives here on the summer solstice."

Laudine strained the elderberry leaves and poured the liquid into a labeled jar. She smiled at Ulla's raised eyebrow and inquisitive expression. "Yes, Bastien is bringing Lukaz here to spend the summer with us while he goes with his sons Gunnar and Haldar to *la Joyeuse Garde,* to train with Lancelot's knights. Normally, Lukaz stays home at *le Château de Beaufort* with his Aunt Gabrielle, since he's too young for the training to become a squire. But now that she has the new babe Ylva to care for, in addition to her three-year-old son Vidar, I thought Lukaz would prefer spending the summer here with us, his paternal grandparents." She wedged a cork stopper into the bottle of elderberry tincture. "Esclados has a magnificent new foal from his stables that he selected as a destrier for Lukaz to ride when he's old enough. In the meantime, Lukaz can learn equestrian skills by riding palfreys with Quentin, our Master of Horse. And I'm hoping that you might help him learn the basics of archery. You're highly skilled with the bow and arrow, Ulla. Would you be willing to teach my grandson?"

Hesitation and fear glimmered in Ulla's apprehensive gaze.

Laudine knew that the gifted healer always avoided babes, new mothers, and young children. Being near them was too painful a reminder of the infant son Ulla had lost three years ago. But Laudine—in her vast experience as a mother and infinite wisdom as a Priestess of the Goddess Dana—knew that helping Lukaz might be the best way for Ulla to heal herself.

Ulla inhaled deeply, as if summoning courage. Raising her expressive green eyes to search Laudine's face, she ducked her chin in solemn, reluctant agreement.

Just as you saved the badly injured Vill, you might heal another wounded little wolf.

My grandson, Lukaz.

Perhaps even my shattered son, Cardin.

Basati. The Basque Wolf of Biarritz.

****

A few days before the summer solstice, Laudine's son Bastien arrived at *le Château de Landuc* with an entourage that included his own two sons, Gunnar and Haldar, his nephew Lukaz, and a dozen knights from *le Château de Beaufort* in Finistère.

As the travelers dismounted, Bastien's knights headed toward the lodging where they would reside until the imminent departure for Lancelot's castle. Quentin, the Master of Horse at Castle Landuc, and several attentive grooms led the horses to the stables.

Laudine hugged Bastien and her three beloved grandsons.

"By the Goddess, how you've grown! You're nearly as tall as I am." She kissed ten-year-old Gunnar's smooth cheek, brushing a curly lock of dark brown hair that so resembled his father Bastien's. "And Haldar, you're as strong as an ox." Golden sunlight gilded her grandson's auburn hair and highlighted his freckled, smiling face. Although two years younger and a bit shorter than Gunnar, Haldar had the broad shoulders and hefty bulk of a future fierce warrior.

Dark brown waves framed the timid little face where eyes as blue as the Breton sea watched Laudine in silent wonder. She held out her arms to the wounded little wolf. And pulled Lukaz into her loving, welcoming embrace. "*Bonjour, mon chou*. By the Goddess, I've missed you. And I am delighted that you'll be here with us for the whole summer." Laudine kissed his six-year-old head and looked up at her husband Esclados, who was greeting the two older boys. "*Papi*," she said, using the French term for grandfather, "could you please bring the boys to see the new colt you've chosen for Lukaz? I'm sure they'd all like to meet him. And I would like to speak to Bastien for a few minutes. We'll come join you at the stables in a little while."

White teeth gleaming against his coppery skin and black hair streaked with grey, Esclados le Ros—the famed Red Knight and Lord of Castle Landuc—beckoned his three young grandsons. "C'mon, boys. Let's go see the fiery Friesian destriers. And meet Lukaz' magnificent foal."

With whoops and shrieks of unbridled glee, Gunnar, Haldar, and Lukaz dashed off to the stables with their robust, laughing grandfather.

****

Alone in the kitchen with her middle son—heir to the throne of Finistère through his royal marriage to Princess Gabrielle, daughter of King Guillemin from *le Château de Beaufort*—Laudine read sorrow and concern in Bastien's troubled gaze as she served him a mug of golden mead. "What's is it, *mon fils*? Please tell me what's wrong."

Bastien took a long pull of the honeyed wine, wiped his mouth with the back of a swarthy hand, and set the silver goblet down upon the oak table. He leaned back in his chair, crossed his sinewy arms over his expansive chest, and sighed in exasperation and grief. "It's Lukaz. He's become withdrawn and despondent. The squires at the castle taunt him, calling him a bastard because he has no father. One of the older boys—with a cruel, vicious streak—accused Lukaz of killing his mother just by being born. Needless to say, that was devastating. Gabrielle and I tried to soothe him, reassure him, but he was inconsolable."

Bitterness and scorn blazed across Bastien's bearded, forlorn face. "And yet—it's the despicable truth, isn't it? Cardin abandoned his son at birth. Because he wrongly blames Lukaz for Charlotte's death." Chiseled jaw clenching with fury and frustration, Bastien lowered his head into shaking hands, raking desperate fingers through his thick, dark locks.

"Lukaz needs his father. And Cardin—as much as he denies it— needs his son to heal his own broken heart." Laudine sipped her chamomile tea and eyed the impassioned face of her loving, generous son. "That's why I've called him home."

Laudine set her teacup down and leaned forward, grasping Bastien's calloused hands. "I swear to you that

I am healthy and hale, but—Goddess forgive me—I am feigning a grave illness. So that Cardin cannot refuse to come home, as he has done every year since Lukaz was born." She smiled at his bewildered expression. "Do you remember Ulla, the young priestess who came here to live when her parents died in Normandy? You were already married then, living in Finistère with Gabrielle at *le Château de Beaufort.* But you might remember the holiday seasons here at Landuc—when Ulla played the harp and sang the most glorious Yuletide carol."

Bastien swallowed a large gulp of mead. "Yes…she had exceptional musical talent and a sublime singing voice. I remember she came back to Landuc a few years ago, when her husband and babe were killed. She'd become mute from the horror. She was living like a recluse in one of the cottages at the edge of the woods. Does she live there still? Why do you ask if I remember her?"

"Because I had her pose as my healer and write a letter to Gaultier, informing him and Cardin that I have a serious illness and have called them both home. I asked Ulla to write that it is my dying wish to have my three sons—and five grandchildren— gathered here at Landuc for my last Yuletide season. But I am not truly ill—it's just a ruse. A necessary lie. To force Cardin to come home. And finally become a father to his abandoned son."

Bastien scoffed, shaking his head in disbelief. "It's a shame you have to resort to such drastic measures just to get Cardin to come home." He downed the rest of his mead, wiped his mouth, and grinned. "But I admire your ingenuity, *Maman.* You've arranged for Lukaz to be here. You've called Cardin home. And you've told everyone that it's your Yuletide wish to have them stay through the holidays. That gives you the rest of the summer, all of autumn, and most of the winter to reunite them. Your clever plan just might work."

He rose to his feet and kissed Laudine's cheek. "I'm going out to the stables to join Papa and the boys. I'm anxious to see this new foal that he's chosen for Lukaz. That's exactly what the boy needs. Something to look forward to. A magnificent horse of his very own. The chance to develop his riding skills. Excel at something. And be proud of himself." Bastien kissed her other cheek with *la bise* of goodbye. "See you soon, *Maman*. *Â bientôt*. I love you. *Je t'aime.*"

****

That evening, Esclados arranged to have his son Bastien and three grandsons—Gunnar, Haldar, and Lukaz—join him and Laudine in the private solar of *le Château de Landuc*. As servants refilled goblets of watered ale for the boys and fine French wine for the adults, an exuberant Lukaz effused about his majestic new colt. "*Papi* says I can ride him in three or four years, when he's strong enough. He's so beautiful, *Mamie*! He's got a glossy black coat and shiny mane. Long, sturdy legs—which means he'll be a fast runner. He's going to be my very own destrier. For when I become a squire. I can't wait to ride him!"

"In three or four years, when the colt is ready, you'll be a more experienced rider, Lukaz. By then, you'll be nine or ten years old. And—with lessons from Lord Quentin, my Master of Horse—you'll be as fine a horseman as your Uncle Bastien. He used to be the Master of Horse for King Guillemin at *le Château de Beaufort*. That's how he met your *Tatie* Gabrielle. But

I'm sure you already know that, don't you?" Esclados affectionately ruffed Lukaz's wavy brown hair, so similar to his father Cardin's dark, thick locks.

"*Oui, Papi*. Uncle Bastien told me that story lots of times before. How he used to give my *Tatie* riding lessons. And he taught her how to wield a sword!" Lukaz took a hearty bite of *manchet*, tearing off an eager mouthful of the finely ground wheat bread with obvious relish.

"That's right, I did. I was her weapons master for several years. Your *Tatie* Gabrielle is descended from Viking Valkyrie, you know. Women warriors who fight as fiercely as men. And I'll teach you, too, Lukaz. You're turning seven this Winter Solstice. That means you'll be old enough to start training to become a knight. And next summer, when Gunnar, Haldar, and I go to *la Joyeuse Garde* to train with Lancelot and his men, you'll come with us, too."

"Sir Lancelot has promised me a warhorse from his stables when I turn fourteen and become an official squire. A robust Percheron, like Papa's horse Drach. I might even get to choose one from the new colts born this summer. I can't wait!" Ten-year-old Gunnar, the oldest of the three boys, beamed, nearly bursting with pride.

"And your horse, Haldar, will be ready to ride next summer. Have you chosen a name for him?" Esclados took a swallow of rich red wine and raised an inquisitive eyebrow as he looked at his auburn-haired grandson.

"*Roux*, because he has red hair. Like me." Amidst a splatter of light brown freckles dusted across his impish face, eight-year-old Haldar grinned from ear to ear.

"Which you got from your mother. I've always

adored Gabrielle's fiery red hair." Lovelight shining in his deep green eyes, Bastien smiled proudly at his young son.

"*Roux* is a fine name for a chestnut Friesian. You chose well, Haldar." The rich timbre of Esclados's deep voice reverberated in the castle solar where with the crisp pine scent of the dense forest wafted in through the two large, open windows.

When they'd finished eating an assortment of sweetmeats and *fruits confits*, Bastien addressed Gunnar, Haldar, and Lukaz. "Tomorrow, after we break our fast, we'll depart at first light for *la Joyeuse Garde*. Boys, kiss *Mamie* and *Papi* goodnight, and go along now with Maëlys. She's got the beds ready for you to sleep. I'll be in shortly to tell you a bedtime story. Tonight, it's the tale of Charlemagne's paladin from the epic poem, *La Chanson de Roland.*"

Amid squeals of youthful delight, the three lads kissed Laudine and Esclados, then followed the chambermaid from the wooden solar, down the dimly lit hall, to the guest bedroom where they would sleep.

Once the boys had left, Bastien spoke quietly to his mother. "You mentioned that Gaultier and Cardin would arrive in August. Since you've called them home because of your grave illness, I would imagine that they'll wonder why I was not summoned back to Landuc to be at your side as well. What will you say to explain my absence?"

"That you'd promised your sons a summer of training at Lancelot's castle. And that Gabrielle— weakened by her recent childbirth—cannot travel with the babe until December. I'll inform Cardin and Gaultier that you'll bring your wife and four children here for the

Yuletide season, just as I requested. And—if all goes as well as I hope—Cardin will have formed a bond with Lukaz by then. And I can proclaim that Ulla, the most gifted healer I have ever trained, has cured me and miraculously restored my health." Laudine raised her wine goblet, prompting the two men to do the same. "To Cardin and Lukaz. May the Goddess reunite father and son at long last."

The next morning, after a hearty meal of porridge with fresh fruit and honey, sliced bacon, poached fish, boiled eggs, and country bread, Bastien and his two sons left *le Château de Landuc* with their dozen knights from Finistère.

"*Au revoir!* See you in December!" Laudine waved goodbye to her departing son and two grandsons, who rode off through the dense Forest of Brocéliande, heading southwest toward *la Joyeuse Garde*, the famed white limestone castle of King Arthur's legendary knight, *Sir Lancelot du Lac.*

"Next year, you'll be riding with them. And begin your training to become a knight." Esclados, standing at Laudine's side, placed a loving, grandfatherly hand upon Lukaz' small shoulder. "Your Uncle Bastien said that you'd like to become a castle archer, like your father Cardin. So, *Mamie* and I thought you might like this fine bow and arrow." He handed Lukaz a taut bow, made from supple yew wood, and a quiver of finely fletched arrows.

Bright blue eyes widened in wonder and delight, Lukaz accepted the gift with a wildly exuberant grin. "My own bow and arrows! *Merci, Papi et Mamie!*" He held the bow, attempted to nock an arrow, and aimed at an imaginary target.

"*Mamie* has arranged for you to develop your skills with a very talented archer named Ulla. She's also an expert huntress, with a magnificent horse and a peregrine falcon. She even has a pet wolf." Esclados chuckled deeply at Lukaz's astonished expression. "*Mamie*'s going to take you to her cottage today so you can meet her and begin your archery training. And maybe—with Ulla as your teacher—you'll become a skilled hunter, too."

****

Laudine watched Lukaz as he sat at the table in the cozy alcove off the castle kitchen, gobbling up the cinnamon oatcakes smothered in honey, licking his chubby fingers with glee. *I am so grateful to have this time with him. I'll lavish him with love and attention. Make him feel wanted and special. With Ulla's archery and hunting lessons, his new bow and arrows, and the colt Esclados has chosen for him, perhaps we can lessen the damage that those heartless squires have done, calling him bastard. Blaming him for his mother's death. By the Goddess, children can be so cruel!*

She sat down at the table with him and sipped a cup of chamomile tea. "When you've finished, I'll bring you to meet Ulla. She lives in a stone cottage at the edge of the woods. She's a gifted healer—she found Vill, her wolf, when he was a wounded pup. His back leg had gotten caught in a rabbit trap, and he couldn't get free. Ulla cut the snare, brought him home, and tended him until his leg healed. She commands him with hand signals and whistles, because she can't talk. Vill is a very well trained wolf. He hunts with Ulla and her falcon, Finn."

Lukaz finished his oatcake and gulped down his

watered ale. He set the mug down on the table, tilting his head to the side as he considered Laudine's words. "She can't talk at all?"

"No, not at all. But she can read and write, so sometimes she communicates through messages that way. But with her hand gestures, she's easy to understand. I think you'll like her very much. She's a skilled archer. A gifted healer. And an exceptional huntress. Her falcon Finn brings down all sorts of high flying birds that arrows can't reach. And Finn can trap rabbits, squirrels, and other small animals with her sharp talons, too. The wolf Vill retrieves the prey and brings it back to Ulla. She feeds Finn and Vill some of the meat, keeps some for herself, and cures the rabbit pelts for the fur." Laudine finished her herbal *tisane* and stood to collect Lukaz' plate and mug. "Are you ready to go out to the cottage and meet Ulla and Vill?"

Lukaz jumped to his feet, blue eyes sparkling like a sun-kissed river in the early morning light. "*Oui, Mamie! Let's go. Allons-y!*"

Chapter 8

Huntress and Healer

"Ulla, I'd like you to meet my grandson, Lukaz. My youngest son Cardin's little boy." Laudine smiled down at the shy lad standing at her side who was nervously trying to hide behind her full skirts. Resting an affectionate, reassuring hand on his hesitant shoulder, she introduced Lukaz to the dark-haired priestess who greeted them on the doorstep of her secluded woodland cottage.

"I've told Lukaz you're a skilled archer," Laudine continued cheerfully, "and that I've arranged for him to have lessons with you each morning." She smiled encouragingly into her grandson's big blue eyes where anxiety warred with wonder. "Lukaz wants to become a castle archer, just like his father. That's why his grandfather Esclados and I have given Lukaz his very own bow and quiver of arrows. So that he's ready to begin his lessons." Laudine indicated the leather case slung across her grandson's back and displayed the weapon he carried, made from the finely crafted wood of a yew tree.

Laudine led Lukaz by the hand as she followed Ulla into the welcoming stone cottage. The wolf Vill lay watchfully on the floor in front of the hearth, eyeing the two visitors warily as he guarded his beloved mistress. "I've also told Lukaz about your wolf. How you healed him as an injured pup and trained him to hunt with you and your falcon Finn."

Ulla nodded at Lukaz, her lovely face alight as she knelt on the wooden floor beside her wolf and stroked his thick grey fur. She raised her eyebrows inquisitively and extended her hand to the little boy, gesturing for him to come forward.

"Would you like to meet Vill? Ulla is offering you the chance to pet him." Laudine grinned at her awestruck grandson. "I wonder if his fur is shaggy or soft? Would you please tell me how it feels? I've never had the chance to get close enough to find out. You must be very special for Ulla to let you touch him."

His chubby cheeks dimpling in delight, Lukaz sauntered forth, exuberant yet still cautious and fearful.

Ulla patted the floor at her side, and the breathless little boy knelt down next to the prone wolf.

Lukaz allowed the young priestess to guide his small hand as he tentatively stroked Vill's dense, wiry fur. "It's rough on the top, *Mamie*," he cried with joyful discovery, "but very soft underneath." Lukas scratched the top of Vill's bristly head and behind the wolf's pointed ears.

Vill affectionately licked Lukaz' fascinated face.

Laudine chuckled softly. "He likes you, Little Wolf."

Lukaz beamed proudly at Ulla as he explained the meaning of his nickname. "My father is called Basati. It means 'savage wolf' in the Basque language of Biarritz, where he lives. That's why *Mamie* called me Little Wolf. Because I'm Basati's son." The youthful, effusive smile—revealing a missing front tooth—quickly disappeared as Lukaz dropped his head in shame. "But all the squires call me 'bastard.' They say I have no father. Because he never comes home to see me."

Compassion and empathy shone in Ulla's forest-green eyes as she glanced up at Laudine.

Cardin is coming home, Lukaz. You'll finally get to meet your famous father. I pray the Goddess melts his hardened heart. And helps me to reunite the two of you at long last.

"Well, perhaps your Papa will come home soon. Maybe even for the Yuletide season." Laudine bent down to hug Lukaz around the shoulders as he continued to pet the wolf. "I'm heading back to the castle now, to prepare my herbs. Lady Ulla will give you your first archery lesson. And bring you out to the castle stables to meet her horse, Nåde. You can show her the colt *Papi* has chosen for you. The beautiful black Friesian. Maybe Lady Ulla will let you ride Nåde with her when she goes hunting with her falcon, Finn." Laudine searched Ulla's face and smiled with relief when the healer nodded in confirmation.

Lukaz rose to his feet and hugged Laudine around the hips. "Thank you for bringing me here, *Mamie*. I like Lady Ulla and Vill."

Laudine's heart soared like a lark. She smiled at Ulla. "Will you please bring him back to the castle when the hunting lessons are done?"

Ulla nodded as Laudine kissed Lukaz' smiling, dimpled cheeks.

With a fond farewell and friendly wave goodbye, Laudine left the cottage and headed back across the castle bailey toward *le Château de Landuc.*

****

Ulla observed the dark, wavy locks of the little boy's bent head as he stroked Vill's fur.

He longs for the father who rejected him at birth. He's lonely and vulnerable, with few friends. His Uncle Bastien and Aunt Gabrielle have taken him into their loving home, but he's too young to play with his older cousins, Gunnar and Haldar. And too big to play with three-year-old Vidar and the babe Ylva. Like me, Lukaz doesn't fit in and feels closer to animals than people. Well, I'll introduce him to mine. And perhaps help him lessen the pain.

Ulla motioned for Lukaz to follow her into the kitchen where a wild plum tarte that she'd prepared just for him sat enticingly upon the wooden counter. *Laudine told me it's his favorite dessert. We'll have a slice later, when we come back from the hunt.* She showed Lukaz the nearby bowl, which was filled with Vill's food. Rasing her eyebrows and gesturing with her hands, she asked the delighted little boy if he'd like to feed her wolf.

"I can feed him? *Merci beaucoup, Madame*! Thank you, Lady Ulla!" He gratefully accepted the heaping bowl and sniffed at the contents. "Smells like rabbit. Is that what Vill eats?"

Ulla ducked her chin and replied with a friendly smile. She whistled for her famished wolf, who leapt to his feet and dashed into the kitchen, eager for his morning meal.

Lukaz set the dish on the floor. And Vill dove right in.

Ulla walked over to the oak table where Laudine had laid the finely crafted yew bow. She lifted it up, held it at arm's length in her left hand, and nocked one of the arrows to get the feel of Lukaz' new weapon.

Lightweight, but strong. The yew wood was supple and flexible. Perfect for a budding young archer. She handed Lukaz his weapon with a hearty nod of approval.

Pride of ownership illuminated his youthful, innocent face.

Vill, who had devoured every last bite in his now-empty dish, sat on the kitchen floor, contentedly licking his chops.

Ulla fetched her own bow and quiver of arrows, chuckling silently as Vill perked up, instantly alert. *He knows we're going outside. He can't wait to romp in the forest.*

With a whistle for Vill and a beckoning gesture for Lukaz, Ulla led them both out the back door of her cottage.

And into the dense Breton woods.

****

Ulla stood behind Lukaz, helping him stand perpendicular to the target she had made and attached to a sturdy oak about five yards away. She demonstrated how to properly hold the bow, nock the arrow, and pull the string back tautly at the level of his eye, keeping his forearm parallel to the ground.

After a few failed attempts, Lukaz released his arrow straight and true, whooping with joy and leaping into the air when it made its mark with a loud, satisfying *thwack.* "I did it, Lady Ulla! I hit the target!" He threw his arms around her waist, hugging her with gleeful abandon.

As she held the jubilant little boy, sharing his unbridled joy, Ulla's spirit soared through the sky like her peregrine falcon Finn. *He is so proud of himself. Archery may very well be exactly what he needs. I am delighted to teach him my skills.*

When Lukaz successfully hit the target several times in a row, Ulla ended the triumphant lesson with silent, positive praise. Clasping Lukaz by the shoulders, she gave him a gentle, encouraging shake, eager nods of approval, and a hearty smile of genuine satisfaction. She then led him up the stone steps into the cottage kitchen, where they left their two bows and quivers of arrows against the wall near the back door. With a grin, she strapped her leather falconry gauntlet to her left wrist, grasped Lukaz by the hand, and dashed back outside to whistle for Vill. When the wolf came bounding through the thicket to join them, she and Lukaz scampered across the castle grounds toward the stables to fetch her Friesian, Nåde.

"*Bonjour,* Ulla! Argant will saddle your horse, so she's ready to go. Is Lukaz riding with you today?" Quentin, the Master of Horse at *le Château de Landuc,* tossed his sandy hair over a shoulder with a freckled, friendly grin. He kissed her hand in greeting and tousled the boy's thick, wavy locks.

Ulla nodded, smiled down at Lukaz, and placed a reassuring hand on his small back.

"Would you like to show the Lady Ulla your foal, Lukaz? The magnificent colt that your grandfather has chosen for you? I'm sure she'd love to see him. He's a black Friesian, just like Nåde." Quentin chuckled at the lad's enthusiastic response to his suggestion. To Ulla, he chortled, "Right this way. The foal is with his mare."

Quentin led a curious Ulla, an exuberant Lukaz, and a cautious Vill to a stable where the Friesian mare nursed her young black foal. The Master of Horse puckered his lips and made reassuring sounds to comfort the mother horse.

"That's my colt, Lady Ulla! *Papi* gave him to me." Lukaz beamed up at her, pride shining in his big blue eyes as he flashed Ulla a gap-toothed grin amid dimpled, chubby cheeks.

"We'll start training him soon, and you can help me. So he gets used to you right from the start. Then, when he's old enough to ride, you'll both be ready. Have you thought of a name for him?" Quentin whistled for the mare to approach, and handed a carrot for Lukas to offer her in greeting.

As she gratefully munched the carrot, Lukaz stroked the mare's forelock and replied to Quentin's question. "Mamie said that Nåde means 'grace' in Lady Ulla's language. I want to give my horse a Viking name, too." He glanced up at Ulla, wonder burning in his bright blue eyes. "Will you please help me name him?"

She stroked the soft, wavy locks of the little boy's dark brown hair and nodded with a delighted smile.

"Perhaps Ulla can write down a few names, and your *grandmère*—the Lady Laudine—can pronounce them for you. Then you can pick the one you like best." Quentin affectionately caressed the mare's nuzzle, and the mother horse returned to her timid foal.

Argant, the capable adolescent groom whose dark hair glistened in the morning sunlight, led a saddled Nåde into the grassy clearing before them. "*Bonjour, Madame.* Hello, Lukaz. Such fine weather today. Perfect for the hunt. And Nåde here is eager to run."

Quentin ducked his chin in gratitude as he accepted the reins from Argant, who waved goodbye and returned to work in the stables. The Master of Horse then helped Ulla climb into the saddle and hoisted Lukaz up to sit before her. "My wife Rozenn is thankful for the ointment you gave her. It's eased the unbearable itch of the skin on her stomach. Thank you, my lady. We're both very grateful."

Ulla was immensely pleased that her knowledge of herbs and skills as a midwife had helped Quentin's young, breeding wife. As he headed toward the stables to return to his horses, Ulla urged Nåde forward with a squeeze of her thighs and a gentle nudge of her booted heels.

"See you later, Ulla. Have fun, Lukaz. *Au revoir*!" Quentin waved goodbye as they trotted off, Ulla's arms wrapped securely around Lukas as she held Nåde's reins, the wolf Vill scampering along at her side.

"Did you like my horse? He's beautiful, isn't he? A black Friesian, just like Nåde." Lukas squirmed excitedly in her arms as he turned his torso to look back at her in the saddle. "Will you help me name him? I want him to have a Viking name. Just like your horse."

Ulla nodded with a grin and hugged Lukas tight. *His enthusiasm and youthful exuberance are contagious. And he is absolutely adorable.*

Wings like those of a tiny sparrow fluttered in Ulla's tender heart.

"Are we going to the castle mews now? To get Finn? *Mamie* said she's a peregrine falcon. And that you're allowed to have one because you're the daughter of a Viking chieftain." Lukas twisted in the saddle to look at her again with widened, beseeching eyes. "Could I please have a falcon, too? My Uncle Bastien is the future King of Finistère. And my Aunt Gabrielle is a princess. That makes me a noble, doesn't it? So I could have a falcon, just like you. Do you think Lord Gauvin could help me train one? And then—when my colt is old enough—I could ride him and hunt with you and Vill and Finn?"

Another excellent means for Lukaz to acquire self-confidence and proficiency in vital skills. I'll train him to become an expert archer. And teach him to hunt.

With bow and arrow. Snares and traps. And a peregrine falcon of his own.

Her expression hopeful yet uncertain, Ulla responded by raising her eyebrows and shrugging her shoulders as if to say, "We'll soon find out."

When they arrived at the wooden aviary where birds of prey were housed in the castle mews, Ulla dismounted and lowered Lukaz from the saddle. She tethered Nåde's reins to a nearby shade tree where the horse could graze under a large canopy of leaves, gesturing for Vill to remain at the Friesian's side and await her return. With a toss of her head, she invited Lukaz to accompany her as she strode up to meet Gauvin, the castle falconer and Lord of the Mews.

"Good day, my lady! Hello, Master Lukaz. Your grandfather mentioned that Lady Ulla would be bringing you on the hunt with her today. Come, I'll introduce you to her falcon Finn." The grey-haired Gauvin led them inside the domed aviary where falcons, hawks, and owls perched on wooden branches at different levels inside the expansive mews. "Here she is, all ready for the hunt."

Finn flapped her broad grey wings and tilted her dark head back and forth in joyful recognition of her mistress.

Ulla strode up to greet Finn, caressing the smooth feathers of the falcon's compact head. As the predator clamped rapacious claws onto Ulla's gloved left wrist, she beckoned for Lukas to come forward and meet her beloved bird.

Ulla's soft whistle informed Finn that Lukaz was a friend, so the falcon allowed him to stroke her fine feathers.

"She does look fierce," the little boy exclaimed with awe, his limpid blue gaze a deep pool of mystery and wonder. "*Mamie* told me that's what her name means in your Viking language." Dark brown waves flew from his imploring face as Lukaz spun toward the castle falconer, who watched with a bemused, patient twinkle in his wise, experienced eyes. "Lord Gauvin, could I please have a falcon, too? Then—when my colt is big enough—I can hunt with Lady Ulla and Finn!"

"As a matter of fact, I do have a fledgling here. She's a peregrine falcon, just like Finn." Gauvin led a fascinated Lukas over to a small perch where a young falcon was tethered by leather jesses strapped around her ankles. "Here she is. Isn't she a beauty?" He stroked the fledgling's head and encouraged Lukas to do the same. "Did you know the females are the best hunters? They're much bigger than the males, who are called *tercels*. The females are more aggressive, too. They're so fast—they swoop down on their prey and strike like lightning, before it can run away." Gauvin reached for a leather falconry glove, raising his eyebrows to ask for Ulla's permission.

She grinned and nodded eagerly, stroking the smooth feathers on Finn's alert head.

Gauvin strapped the leather gauntlet on Lukas' left wrist, then coaxed the young falcon onto the awestruck little boy's extended fingers. "Give her this piece of rabbit meat, so she'll associate you with food. Every day, when you come here, I'll have you feed her. Once she trusts you, she'll be ready to train. In the meantime, you can watch Lady Ulla. She'll show you how she taught Finn. And soon, your falcon can join in the hunt."

When the fledgling finished eating, Gauvin eased her back onto the wooden perch and removed the falconer's glove from Lukaz' hand. "You and Lady Ulla enjoy today's hunt. When you bring Finn back here to the mews, I'll have you feed your little falcon again before you leave." He bowed his head respectfully to Ulla, who led an elated Lukaz outside to rejoin the awaiting horse and wolf.

She released Finn to soar high above, lifted Lukaz into the saddle, and climbed up behind him. With a distinctive whistle for Vill, Ulla hugged Lukaz tight and galloped off into the Forest of Brocéliande.

****

Finn's sharp cry preceded her dizzying dive as she seized a rabbit with razor-sharp yellow talons. Vill darted ahead to fetch the prey and returned to drop the quarry at Ulla's booted feet.

"Finn is so fast! That makes six rabbits. *Mamie* said you use the pelts to make warm clothes for winter. Is that enough fur for a cloak?" Lukaz watched as Ulla bent to retrieve the rabbit, adding it to the others strapped to Nåde's saddle.

Ulla nodded and motioned for Lukaz to climb onto the horse. She boosted him into the saddle, swung her leg over Nåde's muscular back, and whistled for Finn to return to her gloved wrist. She summoned Vill, nudged her horse, and rode back toward the castle mews.

Lukaz' gleeful laughter was joyful music to her fragile, healing heart.

Chapter 9

Lessons

"Mmmm," Lukaz hummed as he took a huge bite of the wild plum tarte Ulla had made just for him. "*Tarte aux mirabelles* is my favorite! Do you like it too, Lady Ulla?" He licked his lips gleefully, bright eyes sparkling with unbridled delight in the late morning sun as he sat at the table in Ulla's cheerful cottage kitchen.

She nodded in agreement, slipping a delectable spoonful of the sweet green plums into her mouth with a satisfied smile. *He loves the pie, just as Laudine said he would. I am so glad I baked it!*

When he'd finished a second slice, Ulla brought the two earthenware bowls and pewter spoons to the kitchen counter, rinsed them in a wooden bucket of water, and dried the dishes and utensils with a soft clean cloth. She placed them in the small wooden cupboard above the counter and returned to the table, smiling at the sight of Lukaz letting her wolf lick his sticky fingers. *It seems Vill loves tarte aux mirabelles, too.*

She placed a tentative hand on the back of Lukaz' head and stroked the soft, dark waves which dusted his small shoulders.

At her touch, the lad looked up at her with large, inquisitive eyes. "Is it time to go back to the castle?"

Ulla ducked her chin and gestured for him to come along.

Lukaz rose from the chair, and Vill was instantly alert, eager to follow the little boy anywhere. Ulla mused how the two had already formed a close bond. *These two have become fast friends. Vill's devotion will strengthen Lukaz as much as the archery and hunting lessons. And with his own horse and falcon, Laudine's Little Wolf will become as fierce as Finn.*

Like the wings of her falcon taking flight, Ulla's spirit soared in the cerulean sky.

****

"We saw my colt in the stables, *Mamie*! Master Quentin said Lady Ulla could write down some Viking names for him, and you could read them for me. I want my Friesian to have a Viking name, like Nåde." Lukaz hugged Laudine around the hips, jumping up and down with excitement and enthusiasm.

"Well, that's a fine idea. Ulla has a piece of slate here and some white limestone chalk that she uses for writing. Perhaps she can suggest a Viking name for your new colt." Laudine fetched the items and handed them to Ulla with a soft chuckle.

Ulla wrote a few words on the tablet, which Laudine read aloud.

"*Løper* means runner. Do you like that name?"

Lukas wrinkled his face, and Ulla scribbled again.

"*Mektig*. It means powerful. How about that one?"

The grimace on his face spoke volumes. "I want a short name, like Nåde."

Ulla reflected for a few moments, then scratched another suggestion onto the slate.

"*Kol*. It means dark, like your Friesian's black coat."

Large blue eyes widened in wonder. "*Oui, c'est parfait!* That's perfect. My colt's name is Kol." Lukaz darted a glance up at Ulla. Worry clouded his bright gaze. "But what about my falcon? She needs a Viking name, too."

Ulla grinned and scribbled a name for Laudine to read.

"*Jeger* means hunter. Do you like it?" His grandmother raised her eyebrows as she smiled down at Lukaz.

Wavy brown locks flew as he shook his small head.

Chalk scratched on the smooth surface, and Laudine read the Norwegian word aloud. "*Rask.* It means fast, quick, or rapid. Like your falcon will be when she's grown."

"Yes! My falcon is *Rask,* and my Friesian is *Kol.*" He threw his sturdy little arms around Ulla's waist and nestled a jubilant face against her flat stomach. "Thank you, Lady Ulla. Now my animals have Viking names, just like yours."

Ulla's heart overflowed as she gazed into Laudine's grateful, twinkling eyes.

"You'll have to tell me all about the archery and hunting lesson at dinner. Maëlys has roasted a goose, and we have fresh vegetables from the garden." Laudine lovingly stroked her grandson's soft brown locks. She looked up, suddenly shifting her attention to Ulla. "Would you like to join us? We'd be delighted to have you." Affection evident on her kind, generous face, Laudine waited for Ulla's silent response.

She shook her head, bowing humbly to politely decline the invitation. Scribbling a message on the slate, Ulla handed it for Laudine to read.

"Of course, you must return to the cottage. You need to clean and cure the rabbit pelts from this morning's hunt while they're still fresh. And you have chores that await you as well." Laudine kissed Ulla on both cheeks with *la bise* of farewell. "I'll bring Lukaz for his next lesson on Wednesday morning, then. Thank you very much for making his first experience today so memorable." She smiled down at her adoring grandson. "Say goodbye to Lady Ulla. We're very fortunate to have an expert archer and huntress to teach you her skills. Just imagine—in a few years, you'll be as fine an archer as your father."

Lukas hugged Ulla's hips with fierce gratitude and affection. "Thank you for teaching me archery and how to hunt. And for the Viking names for Rask and Kol. *Au revoir,* Lady Ulla. See you Wednesday." The little boy knelt on the floor to hug his new furry friend. "Bye, Vill. See you Wednesday."

Vill licked Lukaz' face with loyal lupine affection.

With a wave goodbye and a whistle for her wolf, Ulla exited *le Château de Landuc*, strolled across the grassy castle bailey, and returned to her cottage in the woods.

****

Throughout the summer, Ulla brought Lukaz hunting with Vill, Nåde, and Finn three times each week, returning to the cottage for archery lessons in the late morning. Gradually, as the boy's strength and accuracy improved, she lengthened the distance of the target to further develop his skills.

Lukaz positively glowed with pride as he continued to make excellent progress.

Ulla showed him how to set traps and snares, in

which they caught small birds, squirrels, beavers, and rabbits. Together, they plucked feathers from the fowl, some of which she carefully cut for use as writing quills. Ulla often prepared roasts from the partridge, pheasant, or quail—flavored with wild onions, mushrooms, garlic, vegetables, and herbs from her garden—which the two of them shared in her secluded woodland cottage.

She taught Lukaz how to scrape hides from the squirrels, rabbits, and beavers they trapped, giving most of the meat and bones to Vill, and reserving some for the savory stews they both enjoyed. Cleaning, curing, and drying the pelts, she demonstrated how to prepare the fur, which she used to line cloaks and create hats, gloves, and capes for winter clothing and Yuletide gifts.

On alternate days, Lukaz spent mornings with Laudine, learning to read, write, and calculate numbers. Then, while his *Mamie* instructed the young priestesses studying herbal medicine with her at *le Château de Landuc,* the little boy developed his equestrian skills on gentle palfreys with Lord Quentin, the Master of Horse. By the time the Friesian colt, Kol, was old enough to ride, Lukaz would already be—at nine or ten years of age—an accomplished, proficient horseman.

During the afternoon on days when Lukaz wasn't practicing with Ulla, Esclados le Ros, Lord of Landuc, brought his grandson to the castle mews so that the Little Wolf could train his young peregrine falcon Rask with Sir Gauvin.

With a written note on her tablet, Ulla explained to Lukaz that although Rask wasn't ready to hunt with them just yet, it was essential for the lad to feed and bond with his precious fledgling each time the two of them fetched Finn.

And Sir Gauvin informed Lukaz that once Rask was fully grown, she and Finn could hunt together as a team and bring down larger prey, perhaps even a deer.

"I can't wait until Rask is big enough to hunt with Finn, Lady Ulla. They'll work together and catch even more game for us." Lukaz dropped to his knees, stroking the wolf's thick grey fur as Vill sat impatiently on the grass outside the castle mews, anxious to begin the hunt. The little boy looked up at her with large, inquisitive eyes. "Does Vill like deer meat?"

Ulla laughed silently and nodded vehemently. Vill absolutely adored venison.

Releasing Finn with a flick of her wrist, she hoisted Lukaz onto Nåde's sturdy back, climbed into the saddle behind him, and whistled for her wolf.

And—under the blue Breton sky—galloped off with her eager hunting companions.

****

One afternoon in late August, as the first hint of fall blew in the crisp, pine-scented breeze, Ulla and Lukaz were deep in the forest, retrieving game from the snares they had set the previous day, when she spotted the distinctive white berries of a mistletoe plant hanging from the branches of a majestic oak.

The sacred plant of the Druids. This Yuletide season, the Archdruid Odin will lead his Celtic priests here for la cérémonie du gui—the yearly ritual for cutting the mistletoe. What a treasured find to discover their sacred plant! I'll climb up and cut a small piece to bring back to the castle. And ask Laudine to explain the significance to Lukaz.

Ulla motioned to Lukaz, beckoning him to her side. She pointed up at the clustered ball of the large plant,

69

hanging from a branch of the oak. Gesturing to Vill to sit and stay with the little boy, Ulla withdrew the dagger from her waist and mimicked cutting the plant so Lukaz would understand her intentions. Then, after sheathing her sharp blade, she strode over to the oak, jumped up to grab hold of a low-lying branch, and hoisted herself up into the enormous tree.

While Lukaz watched in wide-eyed wonder from the leaf-strewn ground below, Ulla painstakingly cut a small sprig of the sacred plant, tucked it into her waistband, and lowered herself down to the forest floor. She retrieved the tiny branch from the folds of her dress and handed it to Lukaz.

"What kind of plant is this, Lady Ulla?" He examined the loop shaped foliage and sniffed the round white berries. "It doesn't have a smell."

Ulla motioned toward the castle, trying to convey the message that Laudine—who kept a greenhouse made of glass which permitted her to cultivate plants and harvest herbs year-round—would recognize it and explain the significance to Lukaz.

Comprehension sparkled in his bright blue eyes. "*Mamie* will know what this is. She grows lots of plants and herbs in her *verrière*." Lukaz handed the mistletoe back to Ulla, who smiled encouragingly and nodded in agreement as she protectively tucked the treasured find into the deep green velvet of her gathered bodice.

Together, she and Lukaz retrieved the last two grouse from their snares and reset the traps. Ulla placed the fowl into the straw basket on her arm, whistled for Vill, and led Lukaz back to her stone cottage.

Once inside, she set the basket of fresh game on top of her kitchen counter and covered it with a clean cloth.

Satisfied the grouse could wait until she returned to pluck, prepare, and roast them for dinner, Ulla took an eager Lukaz by the hand and—with Vill bounding ahead through the forest toward the grassy castle bailey—sauntered off toward *le Château de Landuc*.

****

Laudine greeted her effusive, jubilant grandson with an enthusiastic hug, grateful that the archery and hunting lessons with Ulla were progressing so well. During the past three months since Lukaz had begun training with her, he'd formed a closeknit bond with the mute priestess and her beloved wolf. In fact, Laudine mused with a joyful heart, the trio had become inseparable friends.

"*Mamie,* we found a weird plant in a huge oak tree. It was shaped like a ball, with lots of white berries. Lady Ulla climbed up in the tree to cut it. We brought a piece of it here so you could tell me what it is." Lukaz gazed up lovingly at her, adoration and pride sparkling in his bright blue eyes. "You're the High Priestess of Dana. You know *everything* about plants and herbs."

Laudine smiled down upon her Little Wolf, stroking his soft chestnut hair, as Ulla retrieved the sprig of mistletoe from the bodice of her gown. Accepting the berry-laden twig from her former protégée, Laudine remarked, "Mistletoe. Sacred plant of the Druids."

Mouth agape, Lukaz exhaled in audible astonishment.

"Every Yuletide season, Druids search the Forest of Brocéliande for a mistletoe plant such as this," Laudine exclaimed, placing the precious twig in Lukaz' flattened palm. "Once they find it, they tell the Archdruid Odin, who leads the group to the oak tree for the sacred ritual called *la cérémonie du gui*." She beamed at his rapt,

71

awestruck expression. "Odin spreads a white cloth on the ground, and a young, agile Druid climbs the tree and cuts the mistletoe with a special gold sickle. He climbs back down, and Odin gives a portion of the plant to each Druid, to distribute among all the families in our village. We hang the mistletoe over the entrance of our homes. In that way, the sacred plant, tree, and forest—blessings of the Goddess Dana herself—guide and protect us for a prosperous New Year."

Lukaz reverently studied the shiny green leaves and white berries cradled in his hand.

"I think *you* should be the one to show Odin where you found the sacred plant. He will be very grateful. Perhaps he'll even let you be part of the ceremony, since you were the one who found the mistletoe." Laudine hugged her stunned grandson.

"I can lead the Archdruid Odin to the oak tree?" Lukaz' incredulous voice was a breathless whisper. He glanced at Ulla, whose dark green eyes glistened like emeralds in the golden light of the afternoon sun. "But Lady Ulla found the mistletoe plant. *She* should be the one to lead the Archdruid there, not me."

Laudine smiled at the lovely, dark-haired priestess. "Well, I'm sure you can *both* take Odin to the mistletoe plant. After all, you were with Ulla when she found it. That makes you her partner, doesn't it?"

As Lukaz launched himself into Laudine's loving embrace, the sound of horses' hooves, men's voices, and shouting servants caused a commotion at the front of the castle.

Breathless with excitement, Maëlys came running into the kitchen nook, panting with exertion. "Madame, they're just arrived from Aquitaine! Your two sons—and their knights from *le Château de Montmarin* in Biarritz." Cheeks flushed, ample bosom heaving, the plump servant delivered the thrilling news.

"Sir Gaultier and Sir Cardin have come home to Brocéliande!"

Chapter 10

Return to Brocéliande

Eight weeks in the saddle, stopping at night to set up tents, sleeping on the hard, unyielding ground. Sweltering heat in the summer sun, torrential rain and wind, treacherous slippery trails. By the Goddess, he'd be glad to sleep in a bed for the first time in two torturous months. As he and Gaultier approached the familiar forest surrounding *le Château de Landuc*, Cardin was inundated with a fond flood of childhood memories.

Hunting with his older brothers, Gaultier and Bastien. Practicing archery in the dense Breton woods. Felling his first stag. Developing equestrian skills with Sir *Lancelot du Lac*, the trio of brothers spending each summer as lads training with the illustrious First Knight of King Arthur Pendragon. With Lancelot now a close friend as well as former mentor, his brother Bastien brought Gunnar and Haldar—the two oldest of Cardin's three nephews—to *la Joyeuse Garde* every summer solstice for the same purpose.

Guilt washed over him as he thought of his own son. Lukaz.

Cardin had never even seen his boy, let alone trained him or taken him to Lancelot's famous white castle in southern Bretagne.

He's better off living with Bastien and Gabrielle in le Château de Beaufort. When he turns seven—this Winter Solstice—he'll be old enough to begin the training to become a knight. Bastien can bring Lukaz along with Gunnar and Haldar next summer to Lancelot's castle. The three cousins can all train together. Lukaz is far better off without me, a compulsive gambler who wagers his winnings and brawls in every tavern in town. A drunken sot who drowns his guilt in goblets of golden mead. No, I can never be a decent father. I'm no longer a decent man.

In the distance, the enormous barbican defense towers of *le Château de Landuc* rose like impenetrable pillars above the massive oak, birch, and fir trees of the Forest of Brocéliande. As their entourage approached, the watchtower guard—recognizing Gaultier and Cardin, two of the three sons of Lord Esclados le Ros and the Lady Laudine, *châtelains* of the imposing fortress—lowered the drawbridge over the moat, allowing them entrance into the castle bailey.

Quentin, Master of Horse, greeted the arriving travelers, accompanied by his assistant Argant and half a dozen stable hands. As the riders dismounted and handed the reins to the capable grooms, Cardin spotted his father, whose vigorous stride, hearty grin, and firm handshake reflected both his physical strength and parental pride.

"*Bienvenue, mes fils.* Welcome home, my sons." He clasped Gaultier's broad shoulders in a warm, paternal embrace. When he turned to Cardin, tears brimmed in his dark, expressive eyes. "It's been far too long. Your mother will be overjoyed to see you. And grateful that you heeded her call to come home." Brawny arms gripped Cardin in a tight, affectionate bear hug.

Conflicting emotions assailed him.

Guilt. Grief. Shame. Joy.

And when he looked over his father's broad shoulder and saw the adoring amber eyes of his beloved mother, Cardin's knees nearly buckled from the blinding impact.

Wordlessly—as if too overwhelmed to speak—his *maman* wrapped her loving arms around him, resting her head over his thunderously pounding heart.

And he—the broken son, floundering in a tumultuous sea of sorrow and shame—was a little boy once again in the comforting cradle of her maternal embrace. Shuddering and shaking, he succumbed. And melted in his mother's loving arms.

She cushioned Cardin's head upon her shoulder, resting a soft cheek against his bristled one as she tenderly stroked his long, thick hair. "I'm so very glad you've come home. I've missed you terribly, *mon fils. Je t'aime*. I love you, son. As big as the sky."

As big as the sky. Maman always said that when we were young. Her love for her three sons was infinite. Endless. Eternal.

Cardin lifted his head and gazed down at her tender, tear-streaked face. Glorious auburn hair, interwoven with streaks of silver, was gilded by the golden sun. Regret and remorse throttled him in a choking, smothering vise.

Why did I stay away so long? I've missed her so much, yet always denied it. And now, I've finally come home. Just in time to say goodbye. By the Goddess, I've been a fool. Please, let me make it up to her. In whatever time we have left.

Raw emotion rasped her quavering voice. "There's someone who's been waiting to meet you for a very long time. In fact, his whole young life."

Taking him by the hand—like she'd always done when he was just a lad—Cardin's mother coaxed him up the cobblestone path toward the crenelated castle. "Come, Cardin. Meet your son."

Time stood still.

The warm sun kissed his weathered face. A late summer breeze whispered through his long hair. Birds chirped and twittered in the tall trees. The crisp, clean scent of pine mingled with the pungent tang of the freshwater moat.

From the corner of his eye, Cardin glimpsed Sir Olivier de Montfort—First Knight of *le Château de Landuc*—leading the wearied warriors from Biarritz across the grassy bailey toward their quarters in the knights' lodge near the stables. Gaultier and Papa watched with bated breath as he followed his mother, stumbling up the cobblestone path toward the castle entrance.

And there, in front of the massive oak double doors leading into the imposing *Château de Landuc*, stood a dark-haired little boy, his innocent face alight with wonder.

Waiting to meet his pitiful, prodigal father.

"Cardin, this is Lukaz. We call him Little Wolf, after you, Basati—the Basque Wolf of Biarritz." Releasing Cardin's hand, Laudine gestured for the awestruck lad to step forward. "Lukaz, this is your father, Sir Cardin de Landuc, Captain of King Guillemin's royal archers from *le Château de Beaufort* in Finistère. He's been defending the region of Aquitaine, for King Philippe of France, at *le Château de Montmarin* in Biarritz." She stroked Lukaz' dark, shiny waves so like his own. "*Dis bonjour à ton Papa*. Say hello to your father."

"*Bonjour, Papa*." Sturdy little arms tightly encircled his waist as Lukaz flung himself into a clutching, clinging embrace. "I told everyone I'm not a bastard! I *do* have a father. *You.*" He nestled his small head into Cardin's quivering stomach. "I'm so happy you've come home."

Stunned speechless by an onslaught of conflicting emotions, Cardin shook, his stomach clenched, and his throat constricted, as he caressed the boy's soft hair and held him close for the very first time.

His voice raspy and raw, Cardin choked out a muffled response. "Me, too. And I'm pleased to meet you, Lukaz. I'm sorry I've been gone so long."

Enormous blue eyes, filled with hope and desperate longing, looked up at him imploringly. "When you go back to Biarritz, please take me with you. I don't want to live with *Tonton* Bastien and *Tatie* Gabrielle anymore. I want to live with *you*."

Panicked, Cardin searched his mother's rapturous face, pleading for her intervention and his salvation.

"We'll have plenty of time to discuss that later. But first—Lukaz, why don't you introduce Papa to Lady Ulla and Vill?" Laudine laid a gentle hand on the little boy's back, guiding him toward the two companions who waited patiently on the large stone step in front of the castle entrance.

Instantly animated, Lukaz spun toward the intriguing young woman in a deep green dress whose long black curls tumbled to her slender waist. "This is Lady Ulla. She's a Priestess of Dana, like *Mamie*. She's giving me archery lessons, Papa. And teaching me to hunt with her falcon, Finn." He knelt to the ground and hugged a massive grey wolf who lovingly licked his proud, smiling face. "And this is Vill, her wolf. Lady Ulla healed him when he was a wounded pup. She found him caught in a trap. His leg was broken and bleeding. But she healed him, Papa." Lukaz scratched the wiry fur behind the wolf's alert ears. "Vill fetches the game that Finn hunts. He retrieves it for us. Lady Ulla trained him, Papa. And she's helping me train a falcon, too. My very own peregrine. Her name is Rask. Lady Ulla helped me name her. It's a Viking name!"

Laudine chuckled at Lukaz' youthful exuberance. "We can tell your papa all about it once he's had a chance to come inside. Give your Uncle Gaultier a big hug hello, and let's bring him and your papa into the castle. I'm sure they'd like to wash up, change clothes, and have some of Maëlys' delicious *pot-au-feu*. Come, let's bring them both inside."

Cardin followed his mother, his son, the wolf Vill, and the enigmatic Lady Ulla into the castle foyer where afternoon sunlight streaming through the stained glass transom window above the entrance door cast a brilliant palette of colors onto the gleaming pinewood floor.

Memories flooded him. Playing *cache-cache*—hide-and-seek—with his two older brothers. Training with Sir Olivier and the knights of Landuc. Riding his father's magnificent Friesian and Ardennes horses from the renowned castle stables. Summers at *la Joyeuse Garde* with Lancelot and his intrepid knights. Yuletide celebrations, with an adolescent Lady Ulla strumming her golden harp, filling the entire castle with her melodic, angelic voice.

Dancing with his beloved wife.

A smothering blanket of guilt robbed Cardin of breath as his chest compressed with grief.

"Are you all right, Papa?" Blue eyes as bright as Charlotte's searched his face.

Cardin straightened his spine, threw his shoulders back, and inhaled deeply to regain his composure. He cleared his throat and forced a reassuring smile. "Yes, I'm fine. It's been a long time since I've been home."

A dutiful valet descended the stone stairwell which led to the upper two floors of the castle. "Your bedrooms are ready, my lords. I've placed a bucket of warm water in each chamber for you to wash. There's herbal soap, a clean drying cloth, fresh tunic and pair of braies on each of your beds. Shall I escort you upstairs, *messieurs*?"

Cardin glanced at his brother Gaultier, whose eager expression conveyed his impatience to remove the grime and filth from their long journey.

A protective arm resting on Lukaz' shoulder, his mother suggested brightly, "You two go on up to your rooms and refresh. I'll bring Lukaz into the alcove outside the kitchen, where you can join us when you're ready." She kissed her two sons' stubbled cheeks. "See you in a bit. *À bientôt*." With a warm smile, she led Lukaz, Ulla, and Cardin's father, Esclados, toward the castle kitchen. "Maëlys made some oat cakes with cinnamon and honey. Let's have one or two while we wait for your Papa and Uncle Gaultier. Ulla, would you care to join us?"

As he started up the stairs behind his brother Gaultier and the valet Jehan, Cardin noticed that Ulla declined the invitation with a humble shake of her head. She hugged Lukaz, kissed Laudine's cheeks, and whistled for her wolf, who perked up and trotted instantly to her side. With deep green eyes as verdant as the dense forest, she held Cardin's assessing gaze, wordlessly saying goodbye.

And flashed him a dazzling smile that robbed him of coherent thought.

"See you tomorrow, Lady Ulla. For my archery lesson. And the hunt. Bye, Vill!" Lukas waved farewell and happily followed his grandmother to the awaiting treats on the trestle table.

Cardin watched the beguiling dark-haired priestess quietly exit the castle through the back kitchen door, her loyal lupine companion at her heels.

She's breathtaking. Beautiful. But not for you, Basati.

You're a drunken brute. A savage beast.

No woman will ever want the Basque Wolf from Biarritz.

Head bowed in shame, Cardin silently climbed the castle stairs, followed Jehan and Gaultier down the long stone hallway, and escaped into the sanctuary of his solitary room.

****

That evening, as Cardin enjoyed a supper of leek pottage, roast venison, baked trout, and fresh vegetables with herbs from the castle garden, he watched his young son savor the sweetmeats and cherry pastries from the dessert platter and lick his sticky fingers with childish exuberance and obvious relish. "Do you like the honey cakes and *tartelettes aux cerises*? Maëlys is a talented cook, isn't she? I always loved those cherry tarts when I was a boy. Seems you do, too."

"I love them, Papa. But my favorite is *tarte aux*

mirabelles. Lady Ulla made one for me, and it was so good! Maybe she'll make one for you, too." Lukaz took another hearty bite of the fruit pie, smacking his lips with audible appreciation.

"You really like Lady Ulla, don't you, Lukaz? She is a talented archer and huntress. I'm delighted your lessons with her are going so well." Laudine sipped her chamomile tea and smiled sagely at her grandson, her auburn eyes twinkling in the candlelight from the chandelier above the oak table.

"I remember she used to have the most beautiful voice. She'd play the harp and sing Yuletide carols for the entire castle. Yet now it seems she doesn't speak much, if at all." Cardin ducked his chin in gratitude and whispered "*Merci,*" as the valet Jehan refilled his goblet of wine.

"She's mute, Papa. Lady Ulla can't talk anymore." Lukaz regarded him with Charlotte's expressive blue eyes. Pain sliced Cardin like a knife. "But she can whistle for Vill and Finn—her falcon. And she can write messages on her tablet for *Mamie* to read. That's how she helped me pick the names for Kol and Rask."

Cardin raised an inquisitive eyebrow at his mother. "How did Ulla become mute? An injury?"

Reflective and hesitant, Laudine set her ceramic cup of herbal tea down upon the white linen covered table. "She lost her husband, his father and brother, and her infant son in a brutal pirate attack on their *Château des Tourelles* in Normandy three years ago, while you and Gaultier were in Biarritz. Two of her knights helped Ulla escape, and brought her back here to us. She hasn't spoken a word ever since."

She lost her husband, like I lost Charlotte. And her

beloved babe, too. Ulla's entire family has died. No wonder she suffers in silence.

Cardin took a pensive swallow of wine, contemplating Ulla's inconceivable loss.

Across the table, his older brother Gaultier furrowed his brows in concern and voiced the question Cardin wanted to ask as well. "What happened to her husband's castle? Does Ulla plan to return to Normandy?"

His innocent face contorted with anguish, Lukaz shot a terrified glance at his grandmother. "I don't want Lady Ulla to go to Normandy, *Mamie*. I want her to stay here with us."

Laudine reached across the table and comfortingly gripped his little arm. Lovelight shone in her sage eyes as she replied soothingly, "Lady Ulla won't go back to Normandy. She wants to stay here in the Forest of Brocéliande— where she feels safe."

A brusque counterpoint to Laudine's melodic voice, Cardin's father Esclados responded in a rich, deep baritone. "Ulla couldn't go back to *le Château des Tourelles* even if she wanted to. King Philippe sent a legion of royal knights to vanquish the pirates and seize the castle for the French crown. It's extremely valuable because of its location on the bank of the Seine River, which flows directly into Paris. Lady Ulla's husband, Sir Romain de Montreuil, was positioned there to defend the fortress and the bridge for the French king." He swallowed a hearty gulp of wine, wiping his mustached upper lip with a calloused, swarthy hand. "That's why the pirates wanted the castle—to intercept incoming vessels, laden with goods and riches, on their way to King Philippe's royal palace—*le Palais Royal*—on *l'Île de la Cité* in the heart of Paris."

Cardin eyed his gruff father with concern. "What of Ulla's dowry? You said she was the daughter of a Viking chieftain. Surely she must have an inheritance."

"Ulla was twelve years old when her family died. Her dowry—which included vast farmland in Normandy—was seized by the French crown." Bitterness blazed in Esclados' dark eyes as he beheld his incredulous son. "She came to live with us as a young girl then. And has returned as a widow now. She has nothing. That's why she'll remain here at Landuc with us."

"And we're very fortunate to have her. She's a gifted healer. A skilled archer. And an expert huntress." Laudine beamed with admiration for the former pupil she had obviously grown to love. "She's also a furrier and talented seamstress. Ulla cures hides from the animals that her falcon hunts— or the snares she sets in the forest. Many of the villagers pay for her healing services with pelts and skins as well. Ulla uses the fur and leather to craft winter clothing, which she sells at the local market, on festivals, or during jousting tournaments. In fact— that's how she met her husband. He was the champion of the Beltane Joust held here at *le Château de Landuc* four years ago." She smiled nostalgically at Cardin, her voice edged with sorrow. "You and Gaultier were far off in Aquitaine, at *le Château de Montmarin* in Biarritz. But your father, brother Bastien, and Sir Lancelot organized a magnificent three-day joust. And Sir Romain de Montreuil, one of King Philippe's royal knights from Paris, was the champion."

Laudine practically swooned, reliving the romantic, chivalrous tale. "During the joust, Sir Romain wore Ulla's colors—a ribbon of dark emerald green, symbolic of her healing herbs and of the Forest of Brocéliande. He won not only the jousting championship but Ulla's heart as well."

Moved by the stirring memories, Laudine placed a hand over the bodice of her scarlet velvet gown. "Your father and I hosted the wedding here that summer. And Ulla went off with her new husband to *le Château des Tourelles* in the village of Vernon, where Romain and a bevy of royal knights defended the Seine River for King Philippe of Paris. Until the gruesome attack three years ago, when she was brought back to us, stricken mute with grief. She now lives in a stone cottage at the edge of the forest with the wolf she healed as a cub."

Lukaz leapt from his chair, spilling his cup of watered ale with a careless elbow in his effervescent exuberance. "That's Vill, Papa! She healed him, and now he defends her. Like a guard dog." He turned his large, imploring eyes to Laudine. "Can Papa take me to Lady Ulla's cottage for my archery lesson tomorrow, Mamie? I want him to see me hit the target. And come hunting with us, too." He spun toward Cardin, his eager face ablaze with hope. "You can meet Finn, Lady Ulla's falcon. And my peregrine, Rask. Please, Papa? Will you come with us tomorrow?"

Guilt tugged at Cardin as he beheld his bright-eyed young son.

I've been absent his whole life. Such a simple request. But it means so much to him.

As the joy of giving brought an unfamiliar yet welcome warmth into Cardin's cold, cloistered heart, a grin stretched across his grim, bearded face. "Of course. I want to watch your archery lesson. And I love to hunt, too."

Lukaz threw his arms around Cardin's neck and lunged headfirst into his father's awkward, inexperienced embrace. "I'm so glad you came home, Papa. I told everyone I'm not a bastard. I *do* have a father." Tears brimmed in the enormous blue eyes that were so much like his beloved mother's. "*You.*"

Cardin, too overwhelmed to speak, cradled Lukaz against his pounding chest.

And—for the first time in his miserable, wretched life—Basati, the Basque wolf of Biarritz, felt a father's love for his son.

That evening, when Lukaz insisted that his Papa tell him a bedtime story, Cardin regaled his son with a chivalrous tale of how the valiant knights of *le Château de Montmarin* defended Aquitaine against Spanish pirates from Castilla for King Philippe of France. When Lukaz was finally sleeping, Cardin came downstairs to the alcove near the castle kitchen, where his mother Laudine, his father Esclados, and brother Gaultier were enjoying a glass of wine near the crackling fire in the stone hearth.

How do I ask about her illness? Approach the subject of her impending death? I need to know how much time she has left. And how soon I can get back to Biarritz.

Strangely, the thought of returning to Aquitaine did not beckon Cardin with its promise of remote refuge and escape from the painful past. Instead, the idea of leaving Brocéliande and abandoning Lukaz a second time filled him with overwhelming remorse and shame.

He's mercilessly teased for being a bastard because you've been absent his entire life. Are you going to break his heart and abandon him again? Condemn him to a life of ridicule and pain? By the Goddess, Cardin, what kind of father are you?

He accepted a goblet of rich red wine from his father and sat down at the oak table with his parents and oldest brother.

Gaultier spared him the difficulty of broaching the delicate subject. "Maman is being treated by Ulla, who is a gifted *guérisseuse*. Using her exceptional knowledge of healing herbs, Ulla prepares elixirs and tinctures, which she gives *Maman* twice a day." Dark eyes shining with love, Gaultier smiled sadly at Laudine. "We hope *notre mère* will be with us through the whole holiday season."

Laudine reached across the table and squeezed Cardin's calloused hand. "You've made my Yuletide wish come true. Thank you for coming home, son. It means the world to me." She stroked the hair on his knuckles and gazed at him with golden eyes gilded by the candlelight. "Most days, I feel well enough to teach my student priestesses and cultivate the herbs and plants in the glass greenhouse of my *verrière*. But sometimes, I must take to my bed, overcome with fatigue. I pray the Goddess gives me the strength to welcome in the New Year."

Esclados rose from his chair, the greying streaks in his black hair glistening like strands of silver. "Come, my love. It's time for bed. You must rest as much as you can." Helping Laudine to a stand, he bid goodnight to his two sons while his wife kissed Cardin and Gaultier on both cheeks.

"See you in the morning. Lukaz is most anxious for you to watch his archery lesson with Ulla. And join them in the hunt. Goodnight. It's so good to have you home."

Laudine linked her arm though her husband's as Esclados led her away from the table where their two sons finished the goblets of wine.

Cardin watched his parents cross the expansive foyer and climb the stone stairs leading to the bedroom on the upper level. *I've been gone nearly seven years, wasting my life away. Now, I'm finally home, just in time to say goodbye. By the Goddess, I've been a fool.*

The jarring scrape of Gaultier's chair against the wooden floor as he rose to his feet interrupted Cardin's melancholic reverie. "Well, I'm off to bed too. *Morbleu*, it'll be good to sleep on a mattress again! *Dors bien, mon frère.* Sleep well. See you in the morning." He downed his wine, set the empty mug upon the table, and clasped Cardin on the shoulder before heading up the stairs.

Alone with his thoughts, Cardin stared into the fiery embers glowing in the hearth. The haunting image of Ulla danced in the flickering flames.

My mother's healer.

My son's teacher.

A wounded warrior, just like me.

He ducked his chin in gratitude as the servants accepted his empty goblet and cleared the table. Cardin, pensive and solemn, retired to the bedroom of his childhood where he removed his boots, tunic, and breeches.

And dreamt of the beguiling beauty and his forgiving, adoring son.

Chapter 11

A Trio of Wolves

In the alcove of her small kitchen, Ulla stared out the open window where her hens picked at grubs in the dewy morning grass behind the grey stone cottage. She inhaled deeply, relishing the rich, decadent aroma of wild plums which wafted in on the warm breeze. Mingling with the ripe fruity fragrance was the heady floral scent of white *aubépine* blooms tucked amongst the dense hedgerow which enclosed her backyard. She sighed, savoring the moment, before directing her attention back to her task at hand.

She'd just finished preparing an assortment of herbal tinctures, ointments, and elixirs, placing the carefully labeled jars inside the cupboard where she stored her healing supplies. Lukaz would be here soon for his archery lesson. And his father, Laudine's somber son Cardin, would be with him.

Ulla reflected upon the drastic changes in the dashing, debonair knight she remembered from long ago to the sullen, suffering man of the present.

Basati. He's savage, like his name implies. Fierce and feral, like a wolf. Wounded and vulnerable, like Vill was when I first found him. Withdrawn and melancholy, like Lukaz before he began his lessons and met our animals.

The Basque Wolf of Biarritz. A wretched loner who gambles excessively, drinks too much mead, and fights in every tavern in town. So very different from Sir Cardin de Landuc, the finest royal archer for King Guillemin of Finistère.

Just like Vill and Lukaz, Basati needs nurturing care.

As a wave of curative compassion flowed through her, Ulla smiled at the stark realization.

All three of them need me.

A trio of wounded wolves for me to heal.

A knock at the cottage door interrupted Ulla's reverie. She glanced at her yew bow and quiver of arrows leaning against the wall in a far corner of the kitchen. Vill leapt up and dashed to the front entrance, his tail wagging with lupine delight.

Vill knows it's Lukaz. I wonder how he'll behave around Cardin—who perhaps prefers to be called Basati.

With a hand command for Vill to sit, Ulla opened the front door to greet her guests.

Exuberant smile stretching from ear to ear, Lukaz wrapped his arms around her hips and hugged her tight. "*Bonjour*, Lady Ulla! I've brought my Papa to watch me." Dark brown waves framed his pleading face as he lifted his head from her stomach, imploring her with enormous blue eyes. "Can he hunt with us today? When we go to the stables to fetch Nåde, he can borrow one of Papi's Friesians. Or ride his own horse from Biarritz. Please, Lady Ulla? I want him to meet Finn and Rask. Can he come with us? *S'il vous plaît?"*

Ulla chuckled silently, bending down to kiss his soft

cheeks as she nodded her assent. While Lukaz whooped with glee, she glanced up at Cardin, whose deep green eyes held hers. A delicious shiver rippled up Ulla's spine under the intensity of his ardent gaze.

He's an expert archer and skilled hunter. I can tell by the fierce hunger in his eyes.

A bit flustered from the primal aura exuding from Cardin's compelling presence, Ulla welcomed Lukaz and his father into her humble home with a sweep of her outstretched arm.

She noted that Cardin carried a shortbow today, to accompany Lukaz for his lesson. *As a royal archer for King Guillemin of Finistère, he must be highly proficient with a longbow as well. Perhaps he can give me lessons, too.*

The leather quiver of finely fletched arrows slung across his small shoulder, Lukaz gripped his new bow in his right hand, proudly displaying the impressive gift that Laudine and Esclados had given their grandson. With an encouraging smile, Ulla led the little boy and his father into the kitchen where she retrieved her own bow and arrow.

She opened the back door, whistled for Vill, and led Lukaz and Cardin down the three stone steps to the sheltered enclave behind her cottage.

"The target is over there, Papa. On the trunk of that huge tree." Lukaz pointed to a clearing at the edge of the forest where an enormous oak stretched its majestic branches toward the crisp September sky. "At first, I could only reach it from five yards," he explained as he and Ulla led Cardin toward the target. "But now, Lady Ulla moved me back to ten yards. And I can hit inside the rings almost every time. Watch me, Papa!"

Scrunching his face into a grimace of intense concentration, Lukaz aligned himself perpendicular to the target. He nocked his arrow, and—extending his bow to arm's length and keeping his firing arm parallel to the ground—tautly drew the string back to the corner of his tightly pressed mouth. He released the arrow to a superbly satisfying *thwack* as it struck the outer ring of the target.

"Excellent shot!" Cardin boomed with a hearty grin. "Let me show you something that will improve your accuracy." He approached his son and placed his large hands on either side of the boy's torso to straighten his posture. "Beginners often lean back, as you did just now. But if you keep your collarbone parallel to the arrow, your torso straight, and your hips like this," he instructed, positioning them in line with the bow, "your aim will be consistent. And you'll develop accuracy and precision." Cardin stepped back, away from Lukaz. "Now, make those slight adjustments. And try again."

With concentrated effort, Lukaz straightened his torso and aligned his hips. Keeping his collarbone parallel to the arrow, he tightly drew the bowstring back to the corner of his compressed lips for a perfect release. When the arrow struck the inner ring of the target, Lukaz shouted in triumph and jumped for joy. He dropped his bow and hurled himself at his father, who nearly toppled backward from the force of the impact. "*Ça y est*! I did it! *Merci beaucoup, Papa*!" Lukaz buried his head in Cardin's hard stomach, his youthful face aglow with unbridled bliss. "I am *so glad* you came home from Biarritz."

Ulla's spirit soared at the stirring sight of Cardin embracing his young son.

This is exactly what Lukaz needs. His father's love and acceptance. And the priceless gift of his time.

Despite her contentment, a nagging doubt niggled at the back of Ulla's mind.

But what happens to Lukaz when the Basque Wolf Basati returns to Biarritz?

****

Cardin hugged Lukaz tight, sharing the boy's elation at the improved accuracy in his aim due to the slight adjustment in posture. He eyed the intriguing Ulla, who observed them both with a silent, satisfied smile.

She is enchanting and exotic, like a woodland sprite or forest fairy from ancient Celtic lore. A healing aura emanates from her, like heat rising from a flame. The wild, abundant mane of her long black hair reminds me of an untamed horse. And her alluring eyes, full of wisdom and sorrow, beckon with the verdant mystery of a forbidden forest.

"Lady Ulla, it's your turn. Show Papa how you can hit the target, too!" Wide-eyed wonder illuminated Lukaz' face as he beheld his beloved teacher.

With the elegance and grace of a sleek, magnificent horse, Ulla strode away from the enormous oak and positioned her lithe body at a right angle from the target. She shook her luxurious mane of waist-length black curls, straightened her spine and aligned her slim hips. Extending her bow at arm's length from her shoulder, she nocked her arrow, pulled the string back to the anchor point at her chin, and executed a perfect release. With a resounding thud, her swift arrow embedded in the center ring of the target.

Lukaz squealed with delight and hugged Ulla to congratulate her success.

Dark green gown fluttering like foliage in the early autumn breeze, the priestess strolled across the clearing to retrieve her arrow as an animated Lukaz spun excitedly toward his father.

"Papa, show me your skill. Can you hit the target from fifty yards?"

Cardin watched the enticing sway of Ulla's rounded hips as she walked toward the target. Quickly averting his gaze, he responded to his eager son. "Indeed I can. In fact, to become a royal archer at *le Château de Beaufort* for King Guillemin of Finistère, I had to accurately hit a target with my shortbow at a distance of one hundred yards." Cardin chuckled from his belly as the little boy gasped, his rounded mouth agape in awe. "And with my longbow, I had to consistently hit a target at three hundred yards." He grinned at his astonished son, pleased for the opportunity to demonstrate his prowess to Lukaz. And he had to admit that he really wanted to impress Ulla, a fine archer in her own right.

When she approached, having fetched her arrow from the target, her eyes held his with a mesmerizing stare. A shivering thrill rippled up his spine and settled in his pounding chest. He swallowed hard and took a deep breath to calm his racing heart.

With a subtle nod, he stepped back from Lukaz and Ulla. Gripping his superbly crafted bow— made with the heartwood of supple yew on the inside for compression and the sturdy sapwood on the outside for strength— Cardin trudged across the leaf-strewn forest floor to a distance of approximately one hundred yards from the target. As his breathless son and the bewitching priestess watched in wonder, Cardin nocked an arrow, took aim, and executed a perfect release with effortless grace and flawless aim.

Because of its long, triangular fletching and barbed, double-bladed head, Cardin's ash arrow flew swiftly and surely, lodging in the dead center of the target. To show off a bit more for his appreciative audience, he fired two more arrows in quick succession, all three superbly striking and embedding in the innermost circle.

Lukaz leapt into the air, whooping and cheering for his father's impressive feat. When the lad dashed toward the target to retrieve the arrows, the wolf Vill raced eagerly at his side.

A grinning Cardin turned toward Ulla.

And lost all coherent thought in the enticing depths of her dark green eyes.

"Can we go hunting now, Lady Ulla? And fetch Nåde at the stables?" Lukaz proudly returned his father's arrows and looked up at his teacher, beseeching her with bated breath as he anxiously awaited her response.

Ulla smiled at her pupil, her slender hand stroking his soft brown waves. She raised her eyebrows at Cardin, as if to ask, "Are you ready to go?"

"I'll put our bows and arrows inside the kitchen, Lady Ulla." Lukaz slung her quiver of arrows over his free shoulder and took her bow in his left hand. He looked up at Cardin. "Do you want to leave yours here too, Papa? Or bring it with you?"

Cardin preferred to be armed—not only for the hunt, but for potential defense as well. "I'll keep mine. Go ahead and put yours and Lady Ulla's inside the kitchen. We'll wait for you right here."

With Vill at his side, Lukaz dashed across the clearing toward the stone cottage at the edge of the forest.

Cardin watched him disappear inside and reemerge with the wolf a few moments later. He smiled at Ulla. "You've taught him well. He'll become a fine archer. I look forward to seeing the two of you hunt together. I'm anxious to meet the falcons, Finn and Rask. And your Friesian, Nåde. Lukaz talks about her—and you—all the time. Thank you for all you've done for him. My parents and I are most grateful."

Ulla blushed and lowered her eyes as Lukaz and Vill rejoined them.

"All set?" Cardin placed his hand on his son's shoulder. When the lad nodded eagerly, Cardin tilted his head toward the stables with a cheerful grin. "Let's go."

****

"This is Rask, Papa. Lord Gauvin is helping me train her." Lukaz introduced the small peregrine falcon perched on his gloved wrist. The bird observed Cardin with curious, intelligent eyes. "She's too young now, but when she's ready, Lady Ulla and I are going to train her to hunt with Finn!" He handed Rask back to the Lord of the Mews while Ulla fetched her falcon, who flapped her wings, eager for the freedom of flight and the excitement of the hunt.

Cardin marveled as Ulla released Finn into the overcast autumn sky, boosted Lukaz into the saddle, and climbed up behind him. She flashed Cardin a glorious smile and motioned for him to follow. Mounting his own horse—a chestnut Ardennes stallion from his father's renowned stables—he galloped with them through the forest, a joyous Vill bounding along at Ulla's side.

She's an expert rider. And Finn is indeed a fierce hunter. Cardin was mesmerized as the falcon plummeted from the clouds and pulverized her prey with razor-sharp talons clenched like fists. He watched in awe as Vill retrieved the fallen fowl and laid it gently at Ulla's feet for her to place in the satchel. When they'd gathered enough game, the trio of hunters returned to the castle mews, where Ulla fed Finn and Lukaz gave Rask fresh scraps from the hunt.

"She loves rabbit, just like Finn," Lukaz explained to his father as his fledgling tore into the raw meat. "Vill loves it, too. Lady Ulla and I always feed him a full bowl when we get back to the cottage." His bright blue eyes blazed with pride in the late morning light.

The glorious smile on Ulla's beautiful face twinkled in her verdant gaze.

They returned to the stables, where Lukaz confidently stroked the muzzle of his sleek black Friesian colt. "When I'm ten, Papa, Kol will be old enough for me to ride. Then I'll have my own horse when I hunt with Lady Ulla." His flashed a gap-toothed, hopeful grin at Cardin. "Maybe *Papi* will let you keep Kalon," he suggested, indicating the Ardennes stallion Cardin had ridden today. "Then *you* can hunt with us, too!"

Cardin chuckled huskily as he handed the reins to the Master of Horse, Quentin. "We'll see, Lukaz. For now, let's escort Lady Ulla back to her cottage."

"Not yet, Papa. We have to check our traps. Lady Ulla snares rabbits, and she feeds the meat to Vill. Sometimes, she even makes rabbit stew. It's delicious, Papa. Lady Ulla is a great cook!" He beamed at his teacher, who flushed under the praise and lowered her gaze to her brown leather boots. "She's teaching me how to cure the pelts so we can use the fur to make winter cloaks. Come on, Papa. I'll show you where we set our traps." Lukaz dashed off, with Vill bounding exuberantly at his side.

Her pretty face alight with a bemused grin, Ulla led a laughing Cardin away from the stables to follow their ebullient six-year-old guide and his loyal lupine companion.

"That makes eight," Lukaz announced loftily as handed the strung rabbits to Cardin and reset the snares under Ulla's watchful guidance. "Last time, we only caught four." He glanced up at Ulla. "Do we have enough now for Mamie's cloak?"

Ulla raised her eyebrows, smiled and nodded.

"We're making a cloak for Mamie as a Yuletide gift. Lady Ulla is showing me how to sew the pelts together to make a fine fur cloak. It will be beautiful—and keep Mamie warm in the winter. She'll love it, won't she, Papa?" Satisfied with the snares, Lukaz stood, brushed the dirt and crumbled leaves from his grimy small hands along the sides of his woolen breeches, and looked up expectantly at his father.

"I'm sure she will. Especially since it's made with so much love." Cardin ruffled his son's dark hair and met Ulla's enigmatic gaze, where gratitude warred with apprehension. "Shall we head back to the cottage now? I'm sure Vill is famished. And don't forget—you and I promised Uncle Gaultier that we would train with the knights from *Montmarin* this afternoon. Remember?"

"*Oui, Papa.* I can't wait!" Lukaz grabbed Ulla's hand and pulled her toward the cottage. "Come on, Lady Ulla. Let's feed Vill!"

Inside the cottage, Lukaz laid the strung rabbits upon the counter while Ulla retrieved a flat wooden board. Using the dagger strapped at her waist, she carefully scraped the flesh from the hides.

"Lady Ulla cuts the meat off the pelts so we can feed it to Vill. When she's done, we wash the hides in a bucket of soapy water, rinse them off, and let them dry." Lukaz pointed to a few pelts hanging in a corner of the kitchen. "Those aren't ready yet. But these are." He fetched a few rabbit hides from a small table near the drying pelts and brought them over to show his father. "Feel how soft they are. We're going to use them for Mamie's cloak."

After Cardin complied, Lukaz returned the rabbit hides to the tabletop. He hoisted a bucket of water, lugged it across the kitchen, and placed it on the floor at Ulla's side.

With an unexpected pang of jealousy, Cardin wished he could be part of the closeknit bond that Ulla and Lukaz had obviously formed. He watched in amazement as his impressively efficient young son worked closely and collaboratively with the mute priestess.

Lukaz added soap to the bucket of water, stirring with a long handled wooden spoon. He carefully placed the meat-free pelts which Ulla handed him into the frothy liquid. "We have to wash the blood off first," he explained sagely to his bemused father. While Ulla smiled proudly at her expert pupil, Lukaz strode across the kitchen and fetched a second bucket of water, which he lugged with considerable exertion, placing it at his feet beside the first. "Then, we rinse them, like this." He removed the pelts from the soapy mixture and dunked them into the clean bucket, gently squeezing the excess water and placing the fur on the towel that Ulla had laid upon the counter.

Despite the lad's best efforts to avoid spills, Lukaz

had nevertheless slopped soapy water all over the wooden floor. With a soft smirk, Cardin fetched a few drying cloths from the oak kitchen table and knelt down beside his industrious, drenched son. "Here, let me help." He sopped up the mess, wringing the rags over the bucket of soapy water while Ulla laughed silently from the kitchen counter.

"Should we dump the dirty water in the backyard?" Cardin asked as he rose to his feet.

"Yes, and then we can feed Vill!" Lukaz lifted one of the buckets, and Cardin followed his example. They carried the wooden containers out of the kitchen and down the stone steps. Once they'd emptied the contents into the thick overgrowth at the edge of the forest, Cardin and his son returned to rejoin Ulla in the cottage kitchen.

From the wooden cutting board where she had carefully removed flesh from the hides, Ulla used her knife to scrape the portions of rabbit meat into a large ceramic bowl. Enthusiasm sparkled in her emerald eyes as she handed the bowl to Lukaz.

"Papa, you should be the one to feed Vill. Then he'll know you're his friend, too." Lukaz carried the bowl to the corner of the kitchen where the wolf lay on the floor, watching their every move, anxiously awaiting his meal. The lad gave the dish to Cardin, knelt at the animal's side, and scratched the wiry grey fur behind Vill's alert ears. The wolf affectionately licked Lukaz' joyful face.

With a gap-toothed grin, Lukaz looked up at his father. "Let him sniff your hand first, so he'll recognize your scent. Then, set the bowl down in front of him."

Cardin crouched beside his son, cautiously extending his hand to the wolf's enormous maw. He spoke in a calm, reassuring voice. "Good boy, Vill.

Here's some fresh rabbit meat for you." He placed the container in front of the wolf, pulling Lukaz to a stand as he rose to his feet.

"He likes you. Now he knows you're his friend." Lukaz wrapped his arms around Cardin's waist, nestling his head into his father's stomach. "I'm so glad you came home. I love you, Papa."

A wave of overwhelming love and smothering guilt crashed over Cardin as he held his young son. He glanced across the kitchen and met Ulla's expressive green eyes. His throat clenching with remorse and regret, he rasped hoarsely, in a barely audible voice. "I…I love you, too. *My son.*"

Shaken from the onslaught of unfamiliar emotions, Cardin inhaled deeply to regain his usual steely composure. He looked at the little boy who beamed up at him with adulation in his bright blue eyes. "We need to get back to the castle. We promised Uncle Gaultier we'd train with the knights. Let's say goodbye to Lady Ulla and Vill."

Lukaz raced across the room and lunged into Ulla's outstretched arms.

As he watched his son tightly hug the bewitching healer—whose long black curls cascaded around the little boy like a blanket of love— a stark realization struck Cardin like a swift, savage blow to the gut.

She's become a mother to my son.

Withdrawing from Ulla's nurturing embrace, Lukaz dashed back to hug Vill's thick, shaggy coat. "Bye, Vill. I'll see you soon."

Across the kitchen, Cardin held Ulla's verdant gaze, his soul stirring in their entrancing depths. "Thank you, Ulla. I'll bring Lukaz for his lesson Friday morning. I bid

you good day and farewell. *Au revoir, et bonne journée.*"
He turned to address the prone wolf, whose massive head
rested on his enormous front paws. "Goodbye, Vill. See
you soon." With a hearty grin, Cardin led Lukaz out the
back door, down the stone steps, and away from the cozy
cottage at the edge of the woods.

His step light for the first time in many long years,
Cardin traversed the leaf-strewn meadow, crossed the
castle bailey, and returned with his exuberant son to *le
Château de Landuc.*

Chapter 12

Intercepting Ibarra

Andoni Zilar eyed the six shrewd henchmen—his most trusted assassins— seated around the oval table in his oceanfront abode. He patiently waited for his efficient, discreet valets to finish serving the goblets of mead. Once the attendants had retreated from the private solar, he announced the reason for his clandestine summons.

"Comte Eztebe Ibarra departs for Paris in two weeks." Zilar took a long pull from his chalice, wiped his firmly compressed lips, and set the goblet down before him. He rose from his seat, reached for a rolled document lying atop a burled walnut sideboard, and unfurled a map on the oak table. "He will travel northeast from Aquitaine, along this projected route." Retracing the line he'd previously marked on the parchment paper with a long, skeletal finger, Zilar indicated the anticipated path of the importunate Lord of Montmarin. "It will take him approximately six weeks to travel from Biarritz to *l'Île de la Cité* in Paris. He will arrive in early December at *le Palais Royal* to sign the Yuletide Treaty with King Philippe le Bel of France and King Guillemin of Finistère from Bretagne. We must prevent—at all costs—this disastrous Alliance with Aquitaine."

Zilar retook his seat, stretched out his long legs, and crossed sinewy arms over his broad chest. He furrowed his thick, dark brows. "Basati and his brother Gaultier have been called home to Brocéliande. The four dozen knights from *le Château de Beaufort*—sent here by King Guillemin of Finistère—have returned to Bretagne, triumphant in reclaiming Aquitaine for King Philippe of France." Twirling his narrow mustache, he grinned wickedly at the six bearded brutes. "Now is the perfect time to strike."

The crisp saline scent of the sea wafted in on the cool autumn breeze. Irresistible and intoxicating, the lure of *le Château de Montmarin* beckoned Zilar like a siren's song. As the future lord of the oceanfront castle, endorsed and endowed by two majestic monarchs— Edward Longshanks of England and James II of Aragón—Zilar would control all shipping along the Atlantic coast from the north of Spain to the mouth of the Seine. And since the Spanish king also held title as Count of Provence, Count of Barcelona, and Lord of Montpellier, Zilar would profit from all trade along the Mediterranean shores as well.

Everything depended on preventing the disastrous Yuletide treaty.

The dreaded Alliance with Aquitaine.

Between Comte Ibarra of Biarritz, King Philippe le Bel of Paris, and King Guillemin of Finistère.

Zilar hissed like a tightly coiled snake. "You will assassinate Comte Ibarra before he reaches Paris. Here— at *le Château de Tours* in the Loire Valley." He pointed to a designated location on the map. "You'll pose as merchants transporting wine to Paris. I've arranged for you to stop at *le Château de Tours* en route. An entourage of knights who are loyal to Longshanks will accompany you, as if protecting the shipment. But in reality, they will provide additional reinforcement should any unforeseen events unfold." He took another long pull of mead from his chalice. "One of Ibarra's personal guards—Uribe—is a spy for the English crown. He will unlock the door to Ibarra's private quarters, enabling you to slip in quietly, perform the deed, and depart without detection." He scrutinized his men, his steely gaze shifting slowly as he made individual eye contact with each of his adept assassins. "In the morning, Ibarra's body will be found with the wolf head dagger embedded in his back. We'll eliminate Ibarra, prevent the disastrous Alliance with Aquitaine. And Basati will be arrested for the murder."

Zilar shifted his attention to Gizon, the thief who had stolen the bags of silver and the distinctive dagger from Basati in the staged attack behind the Drunken Crow. "Use this weapon." Zilar laid the unique blade with the curved bone handle and the carved head of a massive wolf upon the table. The emerald eye of the snarling beast blazed in the morning sun. "Basati owes Itzal Baroja a hundred pounds of silver. An exorbitant sum that he cannot repay, thanks to the *unfortunate* robbery in the alley near the Drunken Crow." He snickered and downed the rest of his mead. "Spread the word in every tavern in town. Let it be known that Basati in drowning in debt to Itzal Baroja—a staunch supporter of Edward Longshanks and the English king's rightful claim to Aquitaine. When Eztebe Ibarra's corpse is found—murdered by Basati's blade in *le Château de Tours*—it will appear that the Basque Wolf of Biarritz repaid his indebtedness with service rather than silver."

Zilar rang a bell to summon an attendant, gesturing for more mead. Once the competent valet had refilled the goblets and exited the room, Andoni Zilar raised his chalice in tribute. "To your success, my infallible clan. When we eliminate Eztebe Ibarra and successfully thwart the Alliance with Aquitaine, I shall become Lord of Biarritz in *le Château de Montmarin.* And—as the wealthiest shipping merchant in all of France—I shall reward you most handsomely, my intrepid assassins. Beyond your wildest dreams."

****

Dolssa was grateful for the night off from work at the Sultry Siren. Tonight, she'd prepared an *omelette aux champignons* for supper in the tiny kitchen of the room she rented above the tavern. By adding a large cookpot over the hearth and furnishing a corner of her bedroom with a small table and two chairs, she'd created the illusion of a separate kitchen and enlarged the living area within her single space. As she sat at the table by the fire, mending both of her worn homespun gowns, images of Gaultier's handsome face danced in the flickering flames.

It had been weeks since he and his brother Basati had left Biarritz, called home to *le Château de Landuc* in the Forest of Brocéliande. Although she knew it was too soon for a letter to have reached her in Aquitaine, Dolssa kept hoping each day that she would receive news from the man she desperately loved.

Please let me hear from him soon. I pray he'll keep his promise and come back to me. Before my father discovers where I'm hiding.

Dolssa shuddered at the thought. Her overbearing father—Velasco Calderón, Count of Zaragoza—had arranged for his daughter to wed the lecherous, decrepit, and wealthy Vicomte de Toulouse. Horrified by the idea of a forced marriage to the hideous noble, Dolssa had disguised herself as a commoner and escaped with a band of gypsies whose caravan had passed through Zaragoza en route from Barcelona to the Basque coast. For now, safely hidden in the Sultry Siren, she'd managed to elude her arrogant father, who would never imagine his highborn daughter working as a lowly serving wench in a tawdry tavern. Still, she prayed Gaultier would soon return to Biarritz, marry her, and whisk her far away to his native Bretagne.

She sighed wistfully, rising from her chair with the intention of going to bed, when an urgent knock sounded on her wooden door. Dolssa opened it to find Euri—a close friend who also worked at the Sultry Siren—standing beside a strikingly beautiful, curvaceous redhead.

Euri's fair, freckled face was frantic. "Dolssa, we need your help. May we come in?"

"Of course." Dolssa welcomed the pair of visitors into her humble room, closing and bolting the heavy door behind them. "What's wrong?"

"This is Mélisende, the mistress of one of Andoni Zilar's men. She overhead a private conversation with specific details of a planned assassination of Eztebe Ibarra. We must get an urgent message to Gaultier about his brother Basati. The murderous plot implicates him." Euri gave Mélisende an encouraging nod. "Inform Dolssa what you told me."

Amber eyes wide with fright, the auburn-haired mistress whispered, "Count Ibarra left Biarritz a few days ago. He's traveling to Paris—to sign the Yuletide

Treaty between King Guillemin of Finistère and King Philippe of France at *le Palais Royal*." She swallowed forcefully, wiping her palms along the sides of her dress. "I overheard two of Zilar's men say that Ibarra will make a planned stop at *le Château de Tours* in the Loire Valley along the way." Mélisende grasped Dolssa's hands. "Zilar's men plan to kill Ibarra at that castle. With Basati's dagger—the one with the head of the wolf. That will thwart the Alliance with Aquitaine, and Basati will be blamed for the crime."

Dolssa dropped into a chair, stunned by the shocking news. *We must get a message to Gaultier and Basati. But if Ibarra has already left, it will never reach them in time.*

Euri pulled up a chair, sat down beside Dolssa, and took hold of her hand. "I sent a message to Xabi at *le Château de Montmarin*. I told him to assemble the knights in the Great Hall. I asked him to come here, to escort the three of us to the castle. I explained that we have critical news for Sir Aimeric de Tarn, the First Knight of Montmarin who's in charge of the *château* during Count Ibarra's absence. We'll dispatch an urgent message to Gaultier and Basati. And pray that they can intercept Ibarra before it's too late."

Chapter 13

Bonding with Basati

Laudine lay in her mauve velvet canopied bed, gazing at the thick beech trees of the Forest of Brocéliande from her second story alcove window of *le Château de Landuc*.

She felt terribly guilty deceiving her son, but she knew that Cardin would return immediately to Biarritz if he discovered the truth—that she was merely feigning the illness which had forced him to come home, and that she took to her bed each day to keep him here throughout the entire Yuletide season, with the hopes that he would reunite with his estranged son.

Yes, Cardin would be furious indeed if he learned of his mother's deception. He'd storm off to Aquitaine and never speak to her again. Nevertheless, Laudine was willing to take the risk. And so far, the results were paying off. For, despite his outward appearance as the savage, snarling wolf Basati, her brokenhearted, shattered son Cardin was bonding with Lukaz.

And with the lovely, lonely healer, Ulla.

Although Laudine had initially arranged for Lukaz to have archery lessons with Ulla on alternating days, Cardin now brought his son to the secluded woodland cottage every morning for practice. While Lukaz developed his skills as an archer, Cardin taught Ulla to wield the longbow that he had once used himself as an adolescent squire, explaining that it was the perfect height for her.

Several times, as she'd gathered healing herbs in the forest with the young priestesses under her tutelage, Laudine had spotted them practicing, with Cardin's arms wrapped around Ulla to demonstrate proper stance and form. An adept archer already, Ulla was a quick learner. And Laudine was delighted to see her glorious smile return under Cardin's attentive encouragement.

After weeks of diligent training, Lukaz' young fledgling Rask had begun hunting in tandem with Ulla's raptor Finn, the two falcons working together as an efficient team, effectively felling their prey. And, much to Laudine's delight, Cardin now joined Ulla and Lukaz in their daily hunt with the wolf Vill and the two peregrines.

Each afternoon, when father and son returned to the castle, an animated Lukaz regaled Laudine with tales of the raptors' predatory prowess, of the wolf's ravenous hunger, and of the savory stews Ulla prepared with fresh meat from the hunt and aromatic herbs from her garden. Proud of his newly acquired skills in cleaning and curing the hides, Lukaz boasted that he was helping the Lady Ulla create perfect Yuletide gifts from the fine pelts of soft fur.

Laudine watched her withdrawn, introverted grandson flourish under the loving attention of his instructive father and nurturing teacher.

Atop a gentle palfrey from the castle stables, Lukaz improved his equestrian skills each day as he rode with Cardin through the Forest of Brocéliande alongside his grandfather Esclados and Lord Quentin, the Master of Horse. Cardin included his son in the daily intensive training with the chivalrous knights of Landuc and Montmarin, promising to replace the lad's wooden practice sword with a steel blade once Lukaz developed sufficient expertise.

As her Little Wolf was slowly but surely thriving, a grateful Laudine prayed that Cardin—the Basque Wolf Basati—would not abandon Lukaz once again.

Dear Goddess Dana, please help me reach him. Let love heal my shattered son. When Cardin inevitably returns to Biarritz, I pray that he'll bring Lukaz with him. And take Ulla as his Breton bride.

****

Cardin stood at the edge of the forest near Ulla's cottage, a hundred yards from the target he'd attached to the giant beech tree. He admired Ulla's fine form as she drew back the taut bowstring and released the fletched arrow. "Your strength is impressive. Few women would be able to fire a longbow. You'd make a fine castle archer, Ulla."

She flashed him a dazzling smile that took his breath away. Tossing her luxurious mane of long black curls, she strode proudly across the clearing to retrieve her arrows from the target with the sleek, elegant grace of a magnificent Friesian.

"That's what I want to be, Papa! A castle archer, just like you." Arrow nocked, bowstring drawn, Lukaz proudly aimed at his target, but abruptly lowered his weapon. He spun toward Cardin. Worry etched his young, fearful face. "Will you bring me with you when you go back to Biarritz? I don't want to live with *Tonton* Bastien and *Tatie* Gabrielle anymore. I want to live at *le*

Château de Montmarin. In Aquitaine. With *you.*" Tears welling in his forlorn eyes, Lukaz dropped his bow and arrow on the leaf-strewn grass. He flung himself at Cardin, wrapping his little arms tightly around his father's waist in a frantic, desperate hug. "Please don't leave me, Papa. I don't ever want to be called a bastard again."

Cardin cradled his son's weeping head against his hard stomach. He met Ulla's empathetic gaze as she returned from fetching her arrows. In her limpid, deep green eyes, he glimpsed compassion. Sorrow. Suffering.

Instinctively, he reached for her, extending an open palm to invite her in.

Like a whisper of wind, she flew to him. Grasped his beckoning hand. And, wrapping her slender arms around the floundering father and sobbing son, enveloped them both in a quiet, comforting cocoon.

Entwined like vines in the heart of the forest, they clung to each other, interwoven and interlaced.

A thousand conflicting thoughts flowed like raging rapids through Cardin's tortured mind.

I can't bring him with me back to Biarritz. I'm a drunken gambler, drowning in debt. I have no home. No honor. Nowhere for him to live. He's better off with Bastien and Gabrielle at le Château de Beaufort in Finistère.

But Lukaz is miserable there. Mercilessly teased as a bastard. If I abandon him again, it will break him. He'll lose his father. With Maman's impending death, he'll soon lose his beloved grandmother. If he returns to Finistère, he'll lose Ulla, too, the teacher he has grown to love. Her wolf, Vill. The falcons, Finn and Rask. His majestic colt, Kol. All the animals with Viking names he chose with her.

He can bring Rask with him back to le Château de Beaufort. My brother Bastien hunts with falcons. When Lukaz returns here for the holidays each Yuletide season, Papa and Quentin will train him to ride the Friesian. In three years, when Kol is ready, Lukaz can ride his stallion back to Finistère. Serve as a squire to a knight of Beaufort, like Gaultier, Bastien, and I did as lads. Every summer, Lukaz can go to la Joyeuse Garde with his Uncle Bastien and his cousins, Gunnar and Haldar. Train at Lancelot's castle. Just like I did as a boy.

Waves of gut-wrenching guilt washed over him as he came to the stark realization.

Lukaz is better off without me. He'll go back to Beaufort, and I'll return to Biarritz. Win enough silver to pay off Itzal Baroja. And drown my sorrows in an endless sea of glorious, golden mead.

Cardin forced a reassuring smile and glanced down at his young, anxious son. "We'll see, Lukaz. But for now, we need to escort Lady Ulla home. And join Papi and Lord Quentin at the castle stables."

He led Lukaz and Ulla—the vigilant wolf Vill, as always, at her side— through the dense woods, back to the secluded stone cottage. While he watched his son hug the beguiling priestess goodbye, Cardin bid her farewell with a forced cheer he did not feel. "*Bonne journée*, Ulla. See you tomorrow. *À demain."*

His heart as heavy as a bourdon funeral bell, a solemn Cardin brought a silent Lukaz through the thick forest, across the leaf-strewn castle bailey, and back to *le Château de Landuc.*

****

As Maëlys tucked him into bed, Laudine kissed

Lukas goodnight before heading to the private solar to join her husband Esclados, oldest son Gaultier, and youngest son Cardin in front of the hearth. Relaxing in wooden tufted chairs as they imbibed mead, her three men sat companionably in front of the blazing fire, enjoying its lulling warmth against the late October chill.

She accepted a cup of chamomile tea from a competent servant, settled into a comfortable seat, and observed Cardin out of the corner of her eye.

Although Esclados and Gaultier chatted amicably about training with the knights, Cardin scowled in silence and stared into his mug of mead. Brows furrowed into a pensive, brooding frown, he downed the contents of his silver chalice and signaled a valet for more.

Something is troubling him. He's deep into his cups. What happened at Ulla's cottage?

An urgent knock at the door interrupted Laudine's thoughts. When she looked up to see who was calling at this late hour, her heart leapt to her throat at the sight of the crimson-faced stable hand. Hunched over, breath heaving, Argant gasped, "Lady Laudine! Lord Quentin sent me to fetch you." Swallowing forcefully, he stood, inhaled deeply, and spoke in a quavering, anguished voice. "We must hurry, milady. Rozenn's baby is coming. But…there's too much blood!"

Laudine sprang to her feet, wiping damp palms along the sides of her gown. She summoned the dutiful valet who had greeted Argant at the door. "Fetch the Lady Ulla. I will need her assistance for this difficult birth. Tell her to bring the satchel of herbs, and to come with you at once. Go quickly!" As the messenger raced out the door, Laudine mentally calculated what she would need as she spoke to her husband and sons. "I know Ulla does not want to deliver the babe, but I need her skills as a midwife and healer." She turned toward Cardin, whose impassioned eyes blazed in the flickering flames. *He is reliving the night Lukaz was born. When his beloved wife Charlotte died.* "Stay here with Lukaz. If we're not back by morning, bring him to the cottage so he can feed Vill and let Ulla's hens out of the chicken coop." She squeezed his calloused, shaking hand and kissed his bristled, bearded cheek. "I'll send word as soon as I can."

While Esclados and Gaultier strapped on their swords and summoned two additional knights to escort the pair of midwives through the forest, Laudine retrieved her bag of medicinal herbs from the corner cupboard of the alcove in her kitchen. She tucked a needle, thread, beeswax candle, and calendula soap inside the large leather sack. Grabbing a bottle of wine to cleanse potential wounds, she rejoined the men in the castle solar, heading toward the front door just as the valet appeared with a visibly distraught Ulla.

"It's Rozenn's babe," Laudine explained, hooking her elbow inside the healer's slender arm. "I need your help. And your skill. Come, we must hurry." Motioning for her husband, son, and duo of protective knights to depart, she addressed the stable hand Argant. "Lead the way. We'll follow you."

Chapter 14

Rebirth

Carrying a torch to light the way, the stable hand Argant led Laudine, Ulla, and their chivalrous escorts toward the humble cabin nestled in the dense woods not far from the castle stables.

"Send a messenger to fetch us when you're ready to return. Good luck, my love. Rozenn is in very capable hands." Esclados kissed Laudine's cheek, dipped his head to Ulla, and departed with Gaultier and the other two knights, back to *le Château de Landuc.*

When Argant opened the heavy front door of the cabin, Laudine led a reluctant, apprehensive Ulla inside the simple home.

The acrid, coppery stench of blood permeated the foreboding air.

A frantic Quentin, his freckled face crumpled in fear, rushed to greet the pair of midwives. "Thank the Goddess you've come. She's in here." He led Laudine and Ulla into a dimly lit room where a listless Rozenn, her cheeks flushed and feverish, lay whimpering in a bed saturated with blood. Quentin knelt at his wife's side and kissed her limp hand. "Laudine and Ulla are here. They'll help you deliver the babe. Be strong, *mon amour.* Our child will be born soon."

An alarming amount of blood. I'll stanch it with yarrow so I can determine the cause.

"Hello, Rozenn. Ulla and I are here to help bring your babe into the world." Laudine smoothed the damp hair from the young woman's flustered face and spoke in a calm, soothing voice. "I'm going to check you now. Take a deep breath, exhale slowly, and relax."

When the tightening of Rozenn's enormous stomach subsided, Laudine examined her and conferred quietly with Ulla. "She's been pushing too soon. The mouth of her womb has torn. That's why there's so much blood." She glanced at Rozenn, who dozed fitfully between the intense contractions. "I've slowed the bleeding with yarrow and applied herbs to soften the womb and hasten the birth. The herbs work quickly, so she'll be ready to push very soon. Let's replace these blood-soaked linens with fresh ones. It will boost her spirits and renew her strength."

While Laudine rolled up and removed the soiled sheets, Ulla slid fresh ones under Rozenn's feet and legs.

Two hours later, after much coaxing, encouragement, and strenuous exertion, an exhausted but jubilant Rozenn cradled her squalling newborn son. Tears streaming down her sweat-drenched face, she sobbed to her two midwives, "Thank you both so very much. I could never have done it without you."

"You're most welcome, sweetheart." Laudine mopped sweat from Rozenn's sopping brow. "You did very well. But you did tear a bit during the birth, so l need to do a few stitches. Let's give the babe to Ulla. She'll clean him up while I tend to you." Laudine carefully lifted the infant from his mother's embrace and turned to face her former protégée.

Pain and panic flashed in Ulla's widened eyes as Laudine placed Rozenn's newborn son in her trembling arms. Illuminated from behind by the beeswax candle on the wooden table, a shimmering halo bathed the young priestess in soft, incandescent light.

An angel of the Goddess Dana. Laudine's breath hitched at the sublime sight.

While she treated Rozenn, Laudine watched as Ulla lowered her lips to kiss the babe's small head, tracing a delicate fingertip through his dark, abundant hair. The gifted healer gently swabbed mucous from the babe's tiny mouth and nose. She applied an herbal ointment to the cut cord on his small stomach. Folding a clean cloth between his tiny legs, she tucked it snugly around his waist. Finally, Ulla swaddled the babe in a white wrap of softest linen, cradling him close to her broken heart.

When Laudine finished stitching Rozenn's torn skin, Ulla placed the alert, wide-eyed babe into his mother's loving arms. She smiled encouragingly as Rozenn put the infant to suckle at her breast.

After washing her hands in a basin of water, Laudine strode to the doorway and called for Quentin.

The tall, lanky Master of Horse dashed into the room, relief apparent on his haggard, bearded face.

"You have a fine, healthy son," Laudine informed him cheerfully as he rushed to Rozenn's side, bending down to kiss his wife's beaming face and his son's tiny head. "Rozenn will be just fine," she assured him, as she and Ulla packed up their herbal supplies. "She needs plenty of rest, nourishing food, and lots of liquids to replace the blood she lost."

Laudine slung her satchel over her shoulder and nodded to Argant, who disappeared out the front door to fetch Esclados and Gaultier. She smiled at Rozenn, her heart overflowing with joy. "Congratulations, *petite maman.* You're a mother now." She kissed Rozenn's cheek to bid her goodbye. "I'll bc back tomorrow to check on you and the babe. Sleep well. *Bonne nuit.*"

Ulla kissed Rozenn and the baby farewell, a look of desperate longing in her dark emerald eyes.

An effusive, grateful Quentin hugged both midwives and led them to the front door.

When Argant returned with the escorts, Laudine and Ulla left the small, happy family in the cozy cabin and stepped out into the chilly October night.

Slivers of silver moonlight sliced through the dense trees.

"Mother and child are both fine," Laudine informed Esclados as he bent to kiss her cheek. "The babe's a strong, healthy boy." She smiled at her female companion. "Ulla tended to the babe while I cared for Rozenn. I am so grateful for her tremendous help."

Ulla seemed agitated and distraught, for she avoided Laudine's direct gaze and kept her eyes fixed on the ground. Anxious to flee, the young healer darted off, away from the knights headed toward the castle, dashing across the bailey, back to her cottage in the woods.

Laudine exchanged a worried glance with her husband and son as the three of them watched Ulla sprint across the forested ground. "It was extremely difficult for her to hold Rozenn's babe. It must have revived the painful loss of her own infant son."

"Come, you must be exhausted. Let's get you home to bed." White teeth gleaming in the waxing moonlight, Esclados wrapped his arm around Laudine and handed his burning torch to their oldest son. "Gaultier will light the way."

****

In the empty solar of the castle, Cardin drained his goblet of mead and stared into the fire. Fear, guilt, and grief gripped his heart, just as it had nearly seven years ago.

The night Lukaz was born.

As he gazed into the dancing flames, Cardin relived the torturous past.

Charlotte's gut-wrenching screams. Relentlessly pacing in front of the blazing hearth, torn apart by her audible agony. Three excruciating days of labor, as she expended all of her strength to give birth. And finally— on the longest night of the year and the darkest day of Cardin's life—his beloved wife brought forth the child she had so desperately desired.

And sacrificed her precious life for her son.

Cardin buried his face in shaking hands, raking long fingers through his thick, dark locks.

A commotion at the castle entrance interrupted his gruesome memories. When his parents and older brother entered the private parlor a few moments later, Cardin lurched to his feet and rushed across the room to grasp his mother's hands.

Her amber eyes glowed in the golden firelight. "Rozenn and her newborn son are both fine." Concern clouded her clear gaze. "But Ulla is not." The gentle hand that had soothed so many of his childhood scrapes now stroked his bearded cheek. "She needs you, son. Go to her."

Limbs twitching, pulse pounding, Cardin shook as adrenaline surged through his veins.

Tonight, like me, Ulla relived the painful past.

The infant son she lost…and the husband who died defending her.

She and I are alike in so many ways. Tragedy has broken us both.

Ulla is a gifted healer. But she needs healing now.

His voice raspy, rough, and raw, Cardin growled, "I will."

****

An owl hooted from the dense beech trees where splotches of moonlight filtered through the thick foliage. Swiftly and silently, Cardin strode across the leaf-strewn ground as he made his way to Ulla's secluded cottage with the thatched, slanted roof. Dim light illuminated the two mullioned windows flanking the front entrance where twining trails of lush ivy climbed a wooden trellis.

He trotted up the three stone steps and knocked upon the heavy oak door. When Ulla did not respond, he tried the latch and found it unlocked. Cardin let himself in and bolted the door behind him.

In the silent darkness, banked embers glowed in the fireplace along the left wall where Vill reclined on the hardwood floor. Upon Cardin's entrance, the wolf rose to his feet, lumbering forward to greet the familiar guest with lolling tongue and wagging tail.

"Good boy, Vill." Cardin stroked the shaggy fur and scratched behind the lupine ears. Satisfied with the affection and attention, Vill returned to slumber in front of the hearth.

Cardin glanced around the still room. A wooden settee with tufted pillows of rabbit fur and a pair of walnut chairs were arranged in front of the fireplace. Behind the rear wall of the living area, a narrow hall led to two small bedrooms. At the far end of the rectangular interior, a kitchen stretched across the back of the quiet cottage.

Where Ulla stood, bathed in moonlight, staring out the window.

Her body shook with silent sobs, her sniffles the only sound. Slowly and cautiously, as he would approach a wounded animal, Cardin slipped to her side.

She acknowledged his presence with a half turn of her head before fixing her gaze back on the forest. Like glittering stars in the night sky, the tears on her face glimmered in the moonlight.

Cardin gently touched her cheek to wipe one away. He pushed back a wayward lock of long hair which clung to the side of her grief-stricken face. Tenderly, he took her hand, cradled it within both of his own, and raised it to his trembling lips. "Tonight, while you and my mother delivered Rozenn's babe, I relived the night Lukaz was born." He lowered his head to kiss the inner curve of her bent thumb, tucked protectively inside his palm. "The night I lost my wife."

Startled by his intimate confession, her widened eyes darted to his.

He grasped her forearm, gently turning her to face him. In the dark depths of her sorrow, he glimpsed fear, pain, and empathy. "For the past seven years, I've been suffering in solitude. Blaming Lukaz for her death. Shunning my son, living in shame. Drowning myself in drink." He pulled her to his chest, wrapping secure arms behind her shivering back.

Caring compassion glimmered in her gaze as tears spilled down her crumpled cheeks.

With the pad of his thumb, he brushed them away. "And you, Ulla. You've done the same. Shunning others.

Suffering in solitude. Shattered by grief. Just like me." He searched her forlorn face, immersed in her lonely longing. "Tonight, when you held Rozenn's babe…you relived the birth of your own. The son you lost. The husband who died defending you." He tenderly traced her bottom lip with the tip of his thumb. "You and I are the same. Broken. Damaged. Alone."

He lifted her quivering chin. Her sorrowful eyes mirrored the endless mourning of his own empty soul. "You're a healer, Ulla." Lowering his lips to brush softly against hers, he whispered into her open mouth. "Heal us."

Tenderly, he drew her lips into his own, tracing the inner lining with the tentative tip of his tongue. Gently at first, he deepened the kiss, pulling her close as his arms crossed behind her. He leaned her back, one of his hands reaching up into her lush mane of dark curls to cradle her head as he probed every recess of her luscious mouth. Like a dying man slaking his thirst at a cool, crystalline stream, he drank Ulla's flowing essence deep into his desiccated soul.

She came alive in his awakening embrace.

Wrapping her arms behind him, she gripped him tightly in a desperate, clinging hold. She slid her arms under his tunic, running her hands over his flexed back as she caressed the bare, sensitive skin. Helping him remove the garment, Ulla buried her nose in the dark hair across his chest. As if inhaling his scent, she breathed deeply, trailing kisses with warm, eager lips.

Cardin bent to nuzzle her slender throat, sucking at the smooth, delicate skin. When Ulla eased her gown over her shoulders to reveal small, perfect breasts, Cardin's ravenous lips swooped down to suckle the soft nipples with a deep, guttural groan.

She pressed her hips against his hardened length, kissing the skin at the base of his neck as her long fingers stroked the hair upon his pounding chest. Withdrawing from his embrace, she stepped out of her woolen gown as it fell and puddled on the kitchen floor. Limbs visibly trembling, long black curls cascading to her slender waist, a nude Ulla took hold of Cardin's calloused hand.

And—with a gesture for Vill to remain by the hearth—led him to her bedroom down the hall.

****

Moonlight shone through the sheer curtains of the windows on the opposite wall. Ulla stoked the embers in the fireplace on the right and tossed another log atop the crackling sparks. When she turned to face him, Cardin devoured her with ravenous, reverent eyes.

Her creamy skin glistened in the soft, gilded light like a golden, glowing goddess. Longing and fear etched her exquisite face as he pulled her into his sinewy arms. Showering her with soft kisses, he tenderly traced her lips with the tip of his tongue. He parted them to intensify the kiss, exploring the luscious depths of her tempting mouth.

She responded to his taste, her tongue dancing seductively with his. Curious fingers caressed his bare skin as she pulled him close, pressing her hips firmly against his. Her long, lean legs quivered with desire.

He laid her gently upon the bed and removed his boots, braies, and sword. Kneeling over her divine reclining body, Cardin worshipped her with adoring lips. He savored the flavor of her silken skin, the luscious flesh between her lithe thighs.

Throbbing with need, throttled with desire, he

positioned himself between her open legs. Slid trembling hands beneath her rounded bottom. Tilted her receptive hips up. And—with a primal, guttural growl—plunged into paradise.

Ulla wrapped her slender arms around his back, her long legs around his waist, lifting her body to meet his pounding thrusts. Limbs taut with increasing tension, jaw clamped upon his straining shoulder, she soon shuddered beneath him, her molten core clenching his shaft in rhythmic contractions of release.

Cardin erupted into her warm womb, emptying his soul as he filled her with seed.

He held her tight, reveling in ecstasy, shifting his weight slightly so he wouldn't crush her. He peered down into her smoldering, sated gaze. "That was heaven." Her full, sensuous lips beckoned. Brushing them with a tender, reverent kiss, he whispered, "Divine healing—from my golden goddess." A rebirth of his shattered soul.

He lay down beside her, cradling Ulla over his thundering heart. He stroked the glorious mane of her long black curls, inhaling the floral scent of rosewater from the luxurious locks. Now that they'd shared their bodies and seared their souls, Cardin knew he could never leave her.

First, Ulla had healed the wounded wolf Vill.

Then Lukaz, the withdrawn Little Wolf.

And tonight—by bonding with a broken, battered Cardin—Ulla had healed the Basque Wolf of Biarritz.

Chapter 15

Atonement

Ulla awakened to the chirping birdsong of morning larks and an insistent hardness poking and prodding her backside. She parted her legs and welcomed Cardin once again into her warm, willing womb.

With a deep moan, he sheathed himself inside her. He pinned her hips in place, caressing the sensitive bud between her thighs with long, skilled fingers.

Muscles tightening with increased tension like a tautly drawn bow, she catapulted into climax as he arrowed into her, spilling his ample seed.

"A perfect way to start the morning." Cardin kissed the back of her neck and caressed her skin.

Ulla shivered deliciously, rolled toward him, and nuzzled his muscled chest. *I love his chest hair. It's so virile. So primal.* She inhaled his musky, masculine scent, drawing his essence deep into her lungs.

Her heart clenched at the thought of him leaving.

I know he'll return to Biarritz. To the distant land of Aquitaine. But I'm glad we had last night together. Because even after he's gone, I'll have the memory to treasure forever.

As Cardin stretched his long limbs and hummed in satisfaction, she slipped out of bed and scurried into the kitchen to fetch the gown she had dropped on the floor. Quickly pulling it over her head and securing the woven belt at her waist, Ulla stoked the dying embers in the hearth and added more firewood. She stirred some oats into a pot of water, set it over the rekindled flames to boil, and whistled for Vill to accompany her outside. From the chicken coop, she released her hens, plucking the last of the strawberries from the plants tucked among the hedgerow, and headed back to the kitchen, her wolf at her heels.

Fully dressed, Cardin joined her in the kitchen, wrapping his arms around her as he peered over her shoulder. He sniffed appreciatively as Ulla ladled the boiled oats into two ceramic bowls and set them on the oak table. "Mmm…smells like cinnamon." A grin of approval stretching across his scarred, handsome face, he watched as she placed a wedge of cheese, a loaf of meslin bread, several slices of smoked bacon, a jar of honey, and the fresh strawberries near the servings of porridge.

Ulla poured two mugs of ale, handed him a goblet, and gestured for Cardin to break his fast with her.

He dove in with relish. "This is delicious. You're as fine a cook as you are a healer." Admiration glinted in his dark green eyes. While Ulla added strawberries to her bowl of boiled oats and honey, he announced between hearty bites of bread, "I'll fetch Lukaz for his lessons once we've finished." He swallowed a large gulp of ale and wiped the foam from his frothy lip. With a jut of his chin, he indicated an alert Vill and quipped, "Lukaz isn't the only one eager for the hunt."

When they'd both eaten their fill, Ulla collected the dishes and set them on the kitchen counter near a bucket of water. She'd wash them once Cardin left the cottage.

He pulled her into his arms, leaned her back, and planted a passionate kiss on her delighted mouth. "Thank you for the delectable meal. Be back soon with our little archer."

****

As he trudged through the forest, headed toward the imposing *Château de Landuc*, Cardin berated himself for seven lost, lonely years.

I've been a damned fool. Shunning my son. Blaming him for Charlotte's death. Avoiding my family. Drinking, dicing, drowning in debt. I was blind, but these past three months have opened my eyes. It's time for me to atone for my sins. Make it up to Lukaz. Be the father he needs and wants so badly. Spend what little time Maman has left to be the best son I can for her.

Images of Ulla floated to him like a soft, soothing breeze.

Her quiet, calming presence. Her gentle, healing touch. Her divine, welcoming body.

Cardin knew he could never leave her. She was as much a part of him now as Lukaz. The beautiful, beguiling Priestess of Dana had healed both father and son.

He wanted to ask for her hand, but had nothing to offer a bride. Even if Ulla agreed to marry him, he couldn't bring her back to Biarritz. As castle knights, he and his brother Gaultier shared a bedroom at *le Château de Monmarin*. There was simply no room for a wife and child.

How could he possibly provide for a family? He'd returned Charlotte's dowry—including the manor house and lands in Saint-Renan—to her grieving parents. He had no property or inheritance. No title or fortune. No home to offer Ulla and Lukaz.

In a sudden flash of clarity, he froze, transfixed by the dawning revelation.

Gaultier would return to Aquitaine after Maman's death, for he was anxious to rejoin the lovely Dolssa. If Cardin sold the horse he'd ridden from Biarritz, he'd have enough coin to repay Itzal Baroja. He could then send the one hundred pounds of silver with Gaultier back to Aquitaine and eliminate his debt with the ruthless Basque moneylender. And if his other brother Bastien— King Guillemin's appointed heir—agreed, Cardin could resume his position as Captain of the Royal Archers in Finistère.

After all, his assignment to Aquitaine had been voluntary. When Charlotte died, Cardin had requested the distant transfer, eager to escape the constant reminders of the wife and life he had lost. Bastien and Gabrielle had been raising Lukaz as their own ever since, living with her father King Guillemin in *le Château de Beaufort*. After the holidays and Maman's imminent passing, they planned to bring Lukaz back to the castle with them when Cardin inevitably returned to Biarritz.

He could write a letter to Bastien! Explain his desire to marry Ulla. Request permission to return to his position as royal archer for King Guillemin. And provide a home in Finistère for his future wife and son.

Cardin's spirit soared as he skipped up the stone steps and entered the castle.

In the cozy alcove just outside the enormous kitchen—where Maman loved to sip steaming cups of chamomile *tisane*— Cardin spotted his brother, parents, and son breaking their fast at the wooden table under the sunlit window.

Lukaz leapt from his seat, dashed across the room, and flung his arms around his father's waist. "Papa, let's go to Lady Ulla's cottage. I can't wait to see Vill!"

Cardin chortled as he hugged his exuberant son. "We'll go in just a minute." He made eye contact with his parents. "But first, I need to have a word with *Mamie* and *Papi*. Finish your meal with *Tonton* Gaultier. I'll be back in a few minutes when I'm done."

Esclados rose from his seat, his thick brows furrowed in concentration. "We can speak privately in the solar." He helped Laudine to her feet and summoned a dutiful valet. "Mugs of ale for my wife, son, and me."

Once the attendant had seated and served them, he retreated from the solar and closed the heavy oak door behind him.

Cardin took a long pull of ale, sighed heavily, and set the goblet down. He met his parents' worried gaze and confessed with a sad smile, "I wish to atone for the past seven years. Make amends for my grievous mistakes." He reached across the table and squeezed Laudine's soft hand. "I want to be a father for Lukaz. A decent son for you and Papa. An honorable man once again."

Hope shone brightly in her expressive, expectant eyes.

"*Maman*, I wish to marry Ulla, but I can't bring a wife and son back to Biarritz."

She lowered her gaze and stared at the contents in her mug.

"But I have an idea. I'll write to Bastien and request permission to return as a royal archer for King Guillemin at *le Château de Beaufort*. If he agrees—which I believe he will—then I'll have the means to support a family. I can ask Ulla to marry me. And if she accepts, I'll bring my wife and son to Finistère." Eyebrows raised optimistically, he assessed his parents' reaction.

And was thrilled to see unabashed joy spread across their delighted, surprised faces.

"I'll send for parchment and quill. You can pen the letter right now and we'll dispatch the messenger at once. It will take two days to reach Finistère, and perhaps three more to await the response. If all goes well, you'll have your answer next week." Esclados grinned at his blustering, blubbering wife. "Another Yuletide marriage for you to plan, my love. Just like the winter solstice wedding you and Viviane arranged for Bastien and Gabrielle in her glorious Crystal Castle." He kissed Laudine's trembling hand.

"No, Papa—*Maman* is ill. The servants can arrange a simple service for us during the holidays." Cardin wiped away the tears spilling down his mother's smiling cheeks. "We'll stay here with you, *Maman*. Ulla, Lukaz, and I will be at your side. Until the very end."

Laudine cast a conspiratorial glance at her husband before returning her attention to her son. "I, too, wish to atone for my sins." She clutched Cardin's calloused hand, remorse and regret dimming her shining smile. "I pray that you'll forgive me, son, for I have deceived you." Her amber eyes were alight with love and repentance. "I am not truly sick. I feigned a serious illness to force you to come home." Guilt tinged her vibrant voice. "For seven years, you refused to return to Brocéliande. I had to resort to drastic measures." She absently stroked the dark hair on his bent knuckles. "I desperately wanted you to come home. To be here for the holidays. To reunite with your estranged son." Tears brimmed in her loving eyes. "Can you forgive my despicable lie?"

Cardin shot to his feet and pulled his mother into his arms. "Of course I forgive you, *Maman*." He held her at arm's length, scrutinizing her tear-stained, fearful face. "You're certain you're not ill? It's just a ruse?"

She hugged him tight, resting her head over his thundering heart. "I am healthy and hale. And eager to plan a Yuletide wedding for you and your beautiful bride." She reached up to brush a strand of hair from his furrowed forehead. "You've made my Yuletide wish come true. You came home to Brocéliande. You reunited with your son. And you've found love again." Rising up onto her tiptoes, she kissed his bristled cheek. "Ulla healed your broken heart. And you, my savage, lupine son, healed hers."

Esclados opened the door to address Jehan, the attendant waiting in the hall. "Have a courier prepare for immediate departure to Finistère with an urgent message for my son Bastien at *le Château de Beaufort*. Bring parchment, quill, ink, and wax to seal the document. At once."

"*À vos orders, Monsieur.* Right away, sir." Jehan dashed off down the hall. A few minutes later, he reappeared with the required materials and placed them on the table.

Cardin penned the letter to his brother Bastien, blew the ink dry, and rolled up the parchment. He sealed the wax with the imprint of his signet ring and dispatched the royal courier. "Change horses frequently and deliver this message within two days. Await my brother's response, and return right away. Depart at once."

Tucking the sealed message inside his doublet, the

messenger bowed at the waist, turned on his heels, and exited the private solar.

Cardin exhaled in relief and grinned at his beaming parents. "Now, we wait. But in the meantime, I must fetch Lukaz and bring him to Ulla's cottage." Envisioning the beguiling beauty in his arms as she drew back the longbow string, he smirked, "I love the archery lessons as much as my son."

He kissed his mother's cheeks and shook his father's steady hand, his tone now solemn and grateful. "Thank you both for all you've done. I love you very much. I'm sorry it's taken me so long to realize that profound truth."

With a grateful smile, he bowed his head and headed out the door.

Chapter 16

A Yuletide Wish

Rozenn was recovering her strength from the difficult birth. Her newborn was nursing well and thriving. Each time Ulla visited the young mother and cuddled the chubby infant, bittersweet memories of her own son Fjall flooded her with conflicting emotions of anguish and joy.

I was a fool to avoid babes and new mothers. Toddlers and young children. I shunned them, afraid of reviving the pain of my unbearable loss. And yet I find the opposite is true. The maternal love I have for Lukaz— and now for this newborn babe—have filled my empty soul and replaced the desolate grief with a desperate longing for another child.

The late autumn chill nipped at her cheeks as she trudged through the forest, lost in thought. Vill bounded ahead when the cozy stone cottage came into view. The acrid smell of woodsmoke and the savory aroma of rabbit stew wafted from the fireplace into the early evening air.

Her pulse fluttered wildly with anticipation. Cardin would be coming soon.

Every night now, once he'd tucked Lukaz in and told him a bedtime tale, Cardin slipped from the castle and joined her at the cottage. They shared a simple meal, caressed each other in front of the fire, and made love in the moonlight amongst the soft furs in her bed.

Ulla's legs quivered under her woolen kirtle. By the Goddess, she yearned for him. And loved him more and more every passing day.

Each time she melted in his arms, dizzy with desire. Each time he coaxed her to climax with his clever tongue. Each time he poured himself into her and filled her with seed.

Her heart clenched at the thought of him departing for Aquitaine.

He'll leave me soon. When the holidays are over, he'll go back to Biarritz. Lukaz will return to Finistère with Gabrielle and Bastien to begin his official training as a knight. I'll be alone again, like before. But this time, love will nurture my soul. I'll have these treasured memories forever. And perhaps, Goddess willing... Cardin's child.

Thick ivy vines twined up the arched trellis over the entrance of her cottage. She climbed the three stone steps, unlocked the solid oak door, and followed Vill inside. Placing her herbal supplies in the corner cupboard of her kitchen, she leaned against the counter, her throat constricting with sudden dread.

Lukaz would be devastated if Cardin abandoned him again.

Ulla ladled fresh water from a bucket, filled Vill's bowl, and set it on the floor for him to drink. She stared sightlessly at her wolf, seeking a solution.

Perhaps she could convince Laudine to keep Lukaz here at *le Château de Landuc.* He could live in the castle, continue the archery lessons with Ulla every morning, and hunt at her side with Vill, Finn, and Rask.

Supervised by his illustrious grandfather—the renowned Red Knight, Sir Esclados le Ros—Lukaz could begin his formal training as a squire under the tutelage of Sir Olivier de Montfort, First Knight of Landuc, and not be forced to return to ridicule as a bastard whose father had fled once again.

Her hopes gained momentum as her mind raced with ideas.

Quentin, as Master of Horse, could help Lukaz develop advanced equestrian skills. In three or four years—when the Friesian colt was ready—Lukaz would be a proficient horseman, able to ride Kol for the daily hunt with Ulla. Every summer, when Bastien brought his sons Gunnar and Haldar south to train at *la Joyeuse Garde,* Lukaz could join them and learn superior swordsmanship from the legendary *Lancelot du Lac.*

Her spirit soaring like her falcon Finn, Ulla's loving heart overflowed at a tender, endearing thought.

She could be the mother that Lukaz never had.

A knock at the entrance interrupted her reverie.

Ears perked up in alert, Vill dashed to the door and snuffled at the threshold. Recognizing the familiar scent, the wolf's tail thumped against the wall as Ulla let Cardin in.

He swept her into his sinewy arms, swirling her in a dance of joy. "By the Goddess, I've missed you. You've been in my thoughts all day long." As if to prove his point, he pulled her hips against his, pressing the hard evidence against her soft stomach. He nuzzled her neck and kissed her lips. "Something smells incredible." He sniffed the air appreciatively, a wolfish grin stretching across his scarred, handsome face. "Rabbit stew. Let's eat. I'm starved."

Ulla chuckled silently as she led him into the kitchen where a ravenous Vill gnawed furiously on a large, meaty bone. *My wolves are always hungry,* she mused, seating Cardin at the table and pouring two goblets of rich red wine. She handed him a pewter chalice and smiled as he sampled the beverage. *The earthy taste will complement the mushrooms in the stew and enhance the flavor of the meat and fresh herbs.* While he savored the heady wine, she fetched two bowls, two spoons, and a loaf of grainy meslin bread.

Wrapping her hand in a thick cloth, she lifted the simmering pot from the hearth and set it on a rack upon the kitchen counter. Into Cardin's bowl, she scooped three heaping ladles of stew, with two for herself. She served him with an impish kiss and took her place at the table.

He devoured half the bowl with greedy relish, smacking his smiling lips. A roguish glint gleamed in his dark, dancing eyes. "My compliments to the cook." He raised his goblet in tribute. "To another of your culinary delights."

Ulla watched him sop up every last drop of stew with a large hunk of bread. When he'd finished, he licked his fingers and hummed in approval. The deep rumble of his voice rippled up her limbs and settled in her loins.

"That was delicious." He downed the rest of his wine and rose to his feet. Circling behind her chair, he brushed the long hair away from her shoulder and swooped down to nuzzle her neck. "Almost as delicious as you." With the tip of his tongue, he traced her sensitive skin, sucking softly on the lobe of her ear. "I want to taste you, Ulla. Come to bed."

Abandoning the dirty dishes and empty pot on the

kitchen counter, she followed Cardin as he took her by the hand and led her down the hall.

Inside the bedroom, he stoked the banked embers and added another log to the hearth. The crackling fire roared to life and removed the autumn chill from the moonlit room.

Legs quavering, pulse fluttering in her throat, she stood in breathless anticipation as he returned to unlace her bodice and bare her breasts. When his warm lips alternated between each of her aching nipples, Ulla's knees went weak with desire.

He pushed the gown over her shoulders and down her hips, helping her to step out of the dress, which he folded and tossed onto a chair near the bed.

While Ulla stood shivering—and not from the cold November night—Cardin unstrapped his sword, shed his clothing, and laid her gently upon the bed.

"I want to worship your body," he murmured, trailing fervent kisses from her trembling lips to her tingling breasts. As he sucked and tugged on her nipples, the throbbing between her thighs became unbearable. With long, adept fingers, he parted her tender folds. And drove her wild with his wicked, wonderful tongue.

Cardin climbed over her, nudging Ulla's legs apart with strong, impatient knees. Calloused hands slipped under her bottom and tilted her hips up to receive him. As his penetrating gaze pierced her soul, he plunged into her empty, hollow ache. With relentless rhythm he pounded her, like the savage ocean crashing onto a cliff. And when the irresistible waves of release washed over them both, Cardin inundated her with his copious seed.

Sated and euphoric, she exhaled in bliss as he lowered himself to her side. He cradled her head over his thumping heart and kissed her tousled hair. "Come sleep in my arms."

Nuzzling the dark hair on his chest, Ulla inhaled his musky scent deep into her lungs.

She wanted to capture his essence inside her. Keep a part of him with her forever.

As she closed her eyes and drifted off to sleep, enveloped in his protective embrace, Ulla made a fervent Yuletide wish.

That Cardin would change his mind about returning to Aquitaine.

And stay in the Forest of Brocéliande with Lukaz and her.

****

In the alcove off the castle kitchen, Cardin sat with Laudine, Gaultier, and Lukaz, watching his son pour honey over the cinnamon oatcakes fresh from Maëlys' oven. In a few minutes, after the boy had eaten his snack, the two men were planning to take him out to the lists for practice training with the knights of Landuc.

A breathless Jehan abruptly appeared in the doorway. "Pardon the interruption, my lord, but a royal message has arrived from *le Château de Beaufort*." With a reverent bow, the dutiful servant handed Cardin an official document sealed with a crown and three ermine symbols—the royal emblem of King Guillemin of Finistère.

Pulse thundering in his ears, Cardin rose from the oak table and accepted the document with damp palms and shaking hands. He held his mother's intense gaze as he unsheathed the knife at his waist. With a deep, calming breath, he broke the seal. Read the letter. And whooped for joy.

At the inquisitive look on Lukaz' curious face, Cardin decided to choose his next words very carefully. He wanted to ask Ulla for her hand first. If she agreed to marry him, then she and Cardin could tell Lukaz the wonderful news together. If she refused his proposal, Cardin would inform his son when the time was right that he would remain in Bretagne and live hereafter with Lukaz at *le Château de Beaufort* in Finistère.

Cardin grinned at his eager, expectant child, divulging the contents of the letter that were safe to share. "Uncle Bastien will be here for your birthday on the Winter Solstice. He and King Guillemin will arrive on the eighteenth of December. *Tatie* Gabrielle and your cousins will be coming here, too. We'll celebrate your birthday—and the entire Yuletide season—with the royal family of Finistère!"

Beaming with delight, Lukaz finished the last bite of his oatcake and licked the honey from his fingers.

Cardin made eye contact with his brother. "Uncle Gaultier, will you please take Lukaz out to the training field? I need to speak with Mamie. I'll join you both later."

"Of course," Gaultier replied as he rose from his chair. "Come on, Lukaz. Let's get our gear and strap on our swords. I'll help you with your leather armor."

Lukaz kissed his grandmother's cheeks and hugged Cardin goodbye. "*Au revoir, Mamie.* See you soon, Papa. *À bientôt!*"

Once his brother and son had left, Cardin handed the royal document to Laudine and waited with bated breath while she quickly scanned it. "King Guillemin has reinstated my position as royal archer at *le Château de Beaufort*. He's also given me permission to bring my wife and son to live with me at the castle. *Maman*... now that I have a home to offer, I can ask Ulla to marry me. Pray that she says yes!"

Laudine stood, skirted around the table, and pulled Cardin into her loving arms. "Why wouldn't she? She's as besotted with you as you are with her." Amber eyes brimming with unshed tears, she kissed his bristled cheek. "I have something to show you. Wait here. I'll be right back."

A few moments later, his mother returned, clutching a small, intricately carved wooden box with an elaborate metal hinge. She opened it to reveal a pair of golden wedding rings, glistening in the afternoon sun. One was a simple band, etched with a trio of ermine symbols. The other displayed a dazzling, faceted ruby, glittering in the gilded light.

"These were my parents' wedding rings." Laudine's voice was a reverent whisper. "I want you to have them." She placed the box in his trembling hands. The tip of her finger traced the facets of the flawless scarlet gem. "A ruby represents love. Perfect for your beautiful bride." She gazed up at him with a generous maternal smile. "The castle will be filled with love for the holidays. Our whole family will be here." She reached up to stroke the side of his face, her amber eyes aglow. "Bastien and Gabrielle were married eleven years ago on the Winter Solstice—the start of the holiday celebration. We could have your wedding to Ulla here at the castle on the sixth of January. *La Fête des Rois*. Twelfth Night—the culmination of the Yuletide season."

Cardin crushed her against his chest, momentarily too overwhelmed to speak. He gulped in gratitude, kissed her soft cheek, and whispered in her ear. "*Merci,*

Maman. De tout mon coeur. Thank you— from the bottom of my heart." He tucked the jewelry box inside the leather sheath belted at his waist. "I'm going to the cottage to ask her now. If she accepts—can I bring her back to the castle tonight? To announce our betrothal and celebrate?"

Exuberant joy illuminated Laudine's bright face. "Absolutely. I'll have Maëlys prepare a feast!" She turned his shoulders, hastening him toward the door. "Go now. And bring your betrothed back with you."

****

Ulla was sitting at the kitchen table, sewing the fur lining inside the dark green cloak she was making for Cardin as a Yuletide gift, when she heard an unexpected knock at the front door. Lukaz and Cardin had recently gone back to the castle after the archery lessons and morning hunt. From his wagging tail and enthusiasm, Vill obviously recognized the visitor at the door. But Ulla cautiously peered out the window to see who had come to her cottage.

And was stunned to find Cardin standing on her doorstep.

Dashing back to the kitchen table to cover the cloak with a quilt—she didn't want him to see the gift she was sewing for him—Ulla opened the front door and welcomed him in.

Apprehension and elation warred on his scarred, handsome face.

What has he come to tell me? It can't be bad news, for he seems excited. Yet I sense fear in him as well. What on earth could it be?

Plumping the rabbit fur pillows on the wooden settee, she motioned for him to sit in front of the hearth.

He complied, taking hold of her hand to pull her down beside him. Nervous and jumpy, he stroked her hand within his, as if searching for the right words to say.

Cardin swallowed forcefully, a desperate hope in his vulnerable gaze. "I love you, Ulla. I've come to ask you a question that I've been longing to ask for quite some time." He raised her hand to his trembling lips. "I wrote a letter to my brother Bastien, requesting permission to return to my position as castle archer at *le Château de Beaufort* in Finistère."

Ulla's heart leapt to her throat.

"I can't go back to Biarritz.," he stammered, his deep voice quavering. "I could never leave you. Or Lukaz. I love you both too much." He fervently kissed her shaking hand. "I couldn't ask you this before, since I had no home to offer. But now that King Guillemin has granted my request, I can ask you the question that's been burning inside me." He dropped down to one knee in front of her, piercing her soul with his penetrating gaze. "Ulla, will you marry me? Become my wife, and a mother to my son? Come live with us at *le Château de Beaufort* in Finistère?"

She flung her arms around his neck, nearly toppling him to the floor. Tears of joy streaming down her face, she nodded vehemently and kissed his grinning face.

He jumped to his feet, pulled her into his arms, and devoured her lips. "You've healed me, Ulla. Opened my eyes. Reunited me with my son." He gently gripped her face between his calloused hands, showering her with soft kisses. "I'm whole again. Reborn. And happier than I've ever been. I love you and always will. With every beat of my heart."

Cardin retrieved a small wooden box from a pouch

strapped to his leather belt. He opened it and showed her the rings inside. "These belonged to my grandparents. My mother gave them to me for us." He removed a magnificent ruby ring and slipped it on her finger. "It's a bit too big," he remarked, noting the loose fit. "And this one is too small for me. But the local goldsmith can adjust them in time for the wedding."

Ulla's breath caught as he stood and pulled her into his arms.

"*Maman* suggested that we get married on Twelfth Night." He lifted her hand and kissed the ruby ring. "Bastien, Gabrielle, and their four children will be arriving in mid-December, with King Guillemin and his royal entourage as well. The whole family will be here to celebrate Lukaz' birthday on the Winter Solstice." He kissed her smiling, incredulous lips. "We'll feast all through the holidays. Dance, rejoice, and celebrate. And culminate the Yuletide season with a Twelfth Night wedding for you and me."

Her spirit overflowing with joy, she rested her head over Cardin's thundering heart.

He lifted her chin and lowered his lips to hers. Dark eyes aglow with longing and lust, he whispered huskily as he led her toward the bedroom. "Come, *mon amour*. Let's seal our betrothal with love."

Chapter 17

Message for Basati

The vaulted wooden walls of the Great Hall in *le Château de Landuc* were adorned with Yuletide garlands of holly and ivy, the shiny dark green vines interwoven with an abundance of bright red berries and stalks of spicy, aromatic cloves. On the opposite wall facing the elevated dais where Cardin sat at the table of honor with Ulla and Lukaz, a crackling fire heated the vast chamber against the early December chill. Above the mantel of the enormous hearth, fresh evergreen boughs and white hellebore blossoms perfumed the festive air with a sweet floral fragrance and the crisp, clean scent of pine.

Along each side of the room, knights and ladies feasted on frumenty pottage, platters of venison, wild boar, poached salmon and pike, the celebration dinner concluding with sweet tarts and pastries, candied fruits and cheese. As castle servants cleared the tables and refilled goblets of fine French wine, Cardin's father, Esclados le Ros, lord of the castle, rose from his seat to propose a toast.

"*Messieurs, dames*, tonight we celebrate the betrothal of my son, Sir Cardin de Landuc, to the lovely healer, Lady Ulla de Montreuil." The deep baritone of his father's voice reverberated through the great hall.

"They will be married here on the sixth of January. A Twelfth Night wedding—the culmination of our Yuletide season—at *le Château de Landuc*." White teeth gleaming in the candlelight against his coppery burnished skin, the famed Red Knight raised his goblet high, prompting guests to follow his noble lead. "Let us drink to the betrothed couple. To Sir Cardin and Lady Ulla. To their son Lukaz. To their future together as a family in the Kingdom of Finistère."

Amid cheers for the upcoming wedding, lively melodies from viols, rebecs, fiddles, and flutes enticed the jovial celebrants into the adjacent ballroom as musicians began performing and guests began to dance.

While Lukaz remained at the table with his grandmother Laudine, Cardin swept Ulla onto the dance floor to join in *la carole*. Fingers linked with other dancers', they twirled in circles around the room, Ulla's beautiful face alit with silent laughter and sublime joy.

When the evening ended, they tucked Lukaz in bed together. And—while guests retired to their quarters or returned to their nearby homes—slipped quietly from the castle, back to the cottage in the woods.

****

The sumptuous red velvet was perfect. The deep scarlet hue would enhance the dazzling ruby in her exquisite bridal ring. Overwhelmed with gratitude by Laudine's generous offer of the luxurious fabric, Ulla watched in awe as seamstresses sewed the elegant Yuletide wedding gown she would soon wear to marry Cardin.

She and Laudine had just finished preparing herbs and were savoring a cup of chamomile tea in the cozy alcove off the castle kitchen. "The village goldsmith has adjusted the wedding rings. They were delivered this morning." Laudine sipped her steaming *tisane*. "The tailor is creating a gold velvet tunic and black woolen breeches for Cardin to wear. With an elegant black hat adorned with a fine feather plume." Laudine rose from her seat, fetched something from the corner cupboard, and placed it on the table in front of Ulla. Anticipation and excitement widened her expressive eyes.

An ornate bridal wreath—dual strands of ivy and holly were braided with a ribbon of rich red velvet and adorned with sparkling rubies. From the center back of the headpiece, a veil of gossamer golden silk cascaded to the floor. "I created this to match your wedding gown." Laudine placed the wreath on Ulla's head and bent down to kiss her cheek. "You will be a most beautiful bride." She wrapped her arms around Ulla's shoulders and whispered in her ear. "Thank you for healing my son, the Basque Wolf of Biarritz." Tears glimmered in Laudine's grateful gaze. "And my Little Wolf Lukaz, too."

Ulla removed the velvet and silk headpiece, laid it carefully upon the table, and rose to embrace Laudine. *She taught me healing herbs when I was a young priestess. Took me in when my parents died. Welcomed me back when Romain and Fjall were killed. My teacher, my mentor, my friend. And soon—Goddess willing— my mother-in-law as well.*

Amid heartfelt laughter and tears of joy, Laudine rocked Ulla in her loving arms, then released her gently. "Come, let's visit Rozenn and her babe to check on their progress. By the time we return, Cardin and Lukaz will be finished training with Quentin and the horses." Laudine slung her satchel of herbs over her shoulder, and grinned at Ulla. "I hope Maëlys makes a delicious pottage with the pigeons from today's hunt, with fresh rosemary and thyme from my *verrière*."

****

The pigeon pottage was superb. The rich broth was full of carrots, mushrooms, leeks, and onions. The savory herbs perfectly enhanced the tender bits of poultry and the grainy oats. Ulla smiled as she watched Lukaz devour every last bite, sopping up the hearty soup with a large chunk of meslin bread. He licked his fingers, drank several gulps of watered ale, and fixed his large blue eyes on his watchful, bemused father.

"After the wedding, I'm going with you and Lady Ulla back to Finistère? We'll be a family? And live together in *le Château de Beaufort*?" Fragile hope illuminated his bright, eager face.

Seated beside his brother Gaultier at the table in the private solar, Cardin grinned at his young son. "That's right. After the wedding, you, Ulla, and I will travel with *Tonton* Bastien and *Tatie* Gabrielle back to Finistère. I'm returning to my position as royal archer for King Guillemin, We'll be riding home with the king—and four dozen royal knights from *le Château de Beaufort*."

"Can I ride my palfrey all by myself? Master Quentin says I'm ready." Lukaz raised his eyebrows, anxious to earn his father's approval.

"You'll be seven by then. Old enough to begin training to become a knight. Of course you can ride by yourself." Cardin winked at Ulla as Lukaz lunged at him, wrapping his arms around his father's corded neck.

"*Merci, Papa*! I can't wait!" His face beaming with gratitude and relief, Lukaz hugged his father tight. "No one will ever call me a bastard again. Because you'll be with me. And you're my father."

From opposite ends of the rectangular table, Esclados and Laudine smiled wistfully at their grandson just as the valet Jehan appeared in the doorway.

"Pardon the interruption, Lord Esclados, but a bevy of knights await at the castle gate. The leader has identified himself as Xabi Vazquez, from *le Château de Montmarin* in Biarritz. He claims to have an urgent message for Basati." Jehan bowed his blond head respectfully in deference to his lord.

The three men at the table shot to their feet.

Esclados commanded the valet, "Allow them entry and prepare accommodations in the knights' lodge. Have Quentin and Argant tend to the horses. Escort the knights into the castle. Serve them food and drink." Brow furrowed in concern, he glanced at his two adult sons. "We'll receive Xabi's message in the Great Hall."

"*Tout de suite, Monsieur*. Right away, sir." Jehan turned on his heels and rushed off to obey.

Desperation and dread warred in Cardin's intense gaze as he spoke to Ulla and Laudine. "Please tuck Lukaz in bed for me." He turned toward his son. "*Mamie* will tell you a bedtime tale tonight. Papi, Gaultier, and I must meet these men. I'll see you in the morning." He hugged Lukaz, kissed Laudine, and whispered in Ulla's ear, "I don't want to alarm Lukaz, but it must be of vital importance for Xabi to ride all the way from Biarritz. I'll come to the cottage as soon as I can." When Esclados and Gaultier exited the solar, Cardin kissed her and disappeared out the door.

****

Fragrant evergreen boughs and garlands of holly and ivy adorned the huge mantel over the blazing fire which crackled in the enormous hearth. High above the tall stone walls and ogival windows of the castle, candlelight from four chandeliers suspended from the vaulted wooden ceiling illuminated the cavernous Great Hall.

Harried servants with platters of cold meats, cheese, bread, and ale scurried among the two dozen knights from Aquitaine seated at long trestle tables. As Cardin followed his father and older brother through the entrance into the vast chamber, he spotted the familiar armor and long dark hair of his best friend from Biarritz.

When Xabi rose from the table, wiping ale from his mouth, the dire expression on his heavily bearded face sent a ripple of dread through Cardin's shaking limbs. He strode across the room, clasped Xabi in a bear hug, and introduced him to Esclados while Gaultier shook his fellow knight's hand.

Cardin led his weary brother-at-arms to an empty table and motioned for a servant to bring more ale. When Esclados and Gaultier took their seats beside him, Cardin leaned forward to listen to his friend. "Tell me. What message do you bring from Biarritz?"

Xabi accepted a mug of ale from a castle servant and downed half the contents, as if summoning his courage. He set the goblet upon the table and fixed Cardin with an ominous stare. "Eztebe Ibarra is en route to Paris for the Yuletide signing of the Alliance with Aquitaine. He'll stop along the way at *le Château de Tours* on the seventh of December. Where Andoni Zilar's men plan to assassinate him…*with your wolf head dagger.*"

Cardin shot an incredulous look at Gaultier. "Zilar's men must have stolen it—the night of the robbery behind the Drunken Crow."

Xabi nodded and drained the rest of his ale. He fetched a map from a belted pouch at his waist and unfurled it upon the table. With a fingertip, he traced a marked trail from Biarritz to Paris. "This was Ibarra's intended route." Xabi eyed Cardin and Gaultier, his expression grim. "He had planned to arrive at *le Château de Tours* on the seventh of December. But there's heavy flooding along the Loire River to the west, which will force him east to Issoudun." Xabi referred to a spot on the map. "He'll have to stop here at *La Tour Blanche*. The White Tower. I expect Zilar's men will ambush him there."

Gaultier leaned back in his chair, folding long arms on his warrior chest. Battle readiness blazed in his stark, determined gaze. "Then we must get to Issoudun first, prevent the assassination, and deliver Ibarra safely to Paris."

Cardin frowned, pensively rubbing a bristled cheek. "Zilar is allied with Edward Longshanks of England. If he assassinates Ibarra, he stops the treaty, eliminates the Alliance with Aquitaine, and undermines King Philippe of France."

"And—with your dagger in Ibarra's back—frames you for the assassination while he remains blameless in Biarritz." Rage, disgust, and contempt distorted Gaultier's scowling face.

Xabi summarized the urgency of their mission. "We need four days to reach Issoudun. To get there in time, we must leave tomorrow at dawn."

Esclados rose to his feet and spoke to Xabi. "You've ridden hard from Biarritz. I'll provide fresh horses for you and all of your men." He turned to Cardin and Gaultier. "As First Knight, Montfort will remain here with me to defend Landuc. Assemble two dozen knights to accompany you to Issoudun, and gather the supplies you'll need. I'll have Quentin and Argant ready the horses."

Gaultier stood, preparing to leave. He clasped Xabi by the shoulder. "Come, I'll take you and your men to the knights' lodge where you can sleep. In the morning, we'll break our fast here in the Great Hall and depart at first light."

While his brother rounded up the knights of Montmarin who had arrived with Xabi, Cardin spoke quietly to his old friend. "I won't be returning with you to Biarritz after the holidays. I'm staying here with my son Lukaz. And my betrothed, Ulla." He smirked at Xabi's stunned expression. "I'm getting married here at Landuc—on Twelfth Night. I'd be honored if you'd come to the wedding."

A wildly exuberant grin stretched across Xabi's bearded, scarred face. "*Bai, Basati!* Of course I'll be there. I wish you could come to mine as well." In spite of his heavy chain mail armor, Xabi wrapped an affectionate arm around Cardin's shoulder. "Euri said yes. She and I will be married as soon as I return to Aquitaine." With a deep rumble of laughter, he quipped, "Maybe Gaultier will be next. He's fallen hard for Dolssa. And I know she's smitten with him."

Cardin scoffed. "You might be right. Maybe he will." He exhaled and shook Xabi's hand. "Well, I'll see you tomorrow. I've got to explain to Ulla that I'm leaving in the morning. It'll be hard to say goodbye."

Compassion shone in Xabi's dark eyes. "*Bihar arte, Basati.* See you tomorrow." He clasped Cardin's shoulder and joined the procession of knights following Gaultier out of the Great Hall.

"I'll explain to your mother. I'll tell her you and

Gaultier will escort Ibarra to Paris and that—if all goes well—you'll return in time for Lukaz' birthday." Esclados rested a comforting paternal hand on Cardin's shoulder. "Go to Ulla. And, son…" he said, his deep voice quavering, "…rest assured that we'll always take care of them for you."

In case I don't return from Issoudun. Cardin swallowed a tight lump of trepidation. "*Merci, mon père.* Thank you."

****

An owl hooted from his perch in a tall pine. Under the dim light of the waning moon, Cardin wove through the dense trees as he headed toward Ulla's cottage. The warm scent of woodsmoke blanketed the cold night air.

At his knock, she unlatched and opened the front door.

Vill greeted him with a wagging tail and snuffling nose.

Cardin stepped into the welcoming room and scratched the wolf's shaggy fur. He stretched to his full height, pulled Ulla into his arms, and kissed her softly. "That was my best friend Xabi who arrived from Biarritz." He led her toward the wooden settee and settled her in front of the snapping fire. Cardin sat down by her side and took hold of her icy hand. He raised it to his dry lips. "I have to leave in the morning."

She looked up at him like a startled doe, her wide eyes frozen in fear.

"Xabi rode hard from Aquitaine to inform me of a planned assassination of Comte Eztebe Ibarra, the lord he and I both served at *le Château de Montmarin.*" Cardin lowered his gaze to stare at her slender fingers, encircled protectively within his own. He brushed a

153

thumb over her soft skin. "The assassins intend to kill Ibarra with my wolf head dagger—the one that was stolen from me in Biarritz—to make it appear as if I committed the murder." He caressed Ulla's beautiful, frightened face. "Xabi, Gaultier, and I must prevent the assassination. And deliver Ibarra safely to Paris for the signing of the Yuletide treaty, the Alliance with Aquitaine."

Ulla lowered her head and showered kisses over his damp, shaking hands.

Cardin lifted her chin so she would look at him. Tears of anguish glimmered in her forlorn eyes.

"Three dozen of us—all highly skilled knights— will join Ibarra's men. We'll prevent the assassination, escort Ibarra to Paris, and return to Landuc before the Winter Solstice." He cradled Ulla against his chest, stroking her wild mane of long black curls. "Tell Lukaz that I have to go to Paris but I'll be home in time for his birthday." He kissed her rose-scented hair. "Keep him busy with archery lessons and hunting. I'll be back before you know it."

Cardin rose from the settee and pulled Ulla to her feet. He brushed a wayward strand of hair from her terrified face. Parting her lips with a gentle tongue, he whispered into her open mouth. "Come to bed, my love. Let me bid you a proper farewell."

In the silvery moonlight, they made love amongst the soft furs. Desperation fueling their passion, they clung fiercely to each other, tasting and touching, sharing bodies, hearts, and souls.

When Ulla clenched him tightly in climax, Cardin filled her with his love.

And prayed that he would return to wed the woman

who had healed the Basque Wolf of Biarritz.

****

Wrapped in woolen cloaks against the icy December chill, Ulla stood with Lukaz and Laudine in front of *le Château de Landuc,* watching the bevy of knights prepare to depart.

Xabi and his men from Montmarin sat astride their impressive mounts. Cloudy puffs from the horses' impatient snorts formed wisps in the frosty air.

Esclados assisted Quentin, Argant, and the stable hands with the packing of saddlebags and supplies, then strode across the courtyard to join Laudine at Lukaz' side.

Ulla's heart clenched as Cardin climbed into the saddle. He was magnificent. Dark hair cascaded from beneath his metal coif headpiece. Atop the fiery Friesian stallion, his chain mail armor glinted in the early morning sun. A gleaming sword and *bouclier* shield were belted on his left hip. His fine yew bow was securely strapped across his broad back. And the covered quiver of arrows was firmly attached to the leather saddle on his right.

Dear Goddess, please bring him back safely to us. Lukaz and I love and need him so very much. As does the child I now carry in my womb.

With a confident, dazzling smile, Cardin waved goodbye, fell in line with Gaultier and the knights of Landuc, and led the chivalrous *cortège* en route to Issoudun.

Chapter 18

La Tour Blanche

Cardin rolled up the blankets he'd slept on and packed them into his saddle, a numbing chill deep in his bones. Ever since they'd left *le Château de Landuc* four days ago, he, Gaultier, Xabi, and their knights had been sleeping on the cold, hard ground. They didn't dare risk a fire for fear of attracting attention. So they shivered inside their metal armor, trying to keep warm with cloaks and blankets, eating barely palatable dried, salted food. His packing complete, Cardin joined Xabi and Gaultier near their horses as the group prepared to depart camp.

Xabi secured the satchel on his horse's back. "Scouts report seeing Ibarra's caravan approximately eight miles southwest. We'll reach them by midmorning and approach with this banner." He displayed a blue flag with a trio of gold *fleur-de-lys* emblems, symbol of the French monarchy. "They'll know at once that we support King Philippe of Paris. And Ibarra's guards will recognize the surcoats and heraldry of our knights from Montmarin." Xabi folded the flag, tucked it into his satchel, and spoke to both Cardin and Gaultier. "We need to separate Ibarra from the caravan and get him quickly to *la Tour Blanche*. The two of you, take the knights from Landuc, get Ibarra to the Tower, and defend him from attack. I'll take the knights from Montmarin and join Ibarra's guards. We'll defend the valuables inside the carriages as we make our way to the fortress."

Cardin stroked his horse's muzzle to calm the restless stallion. "We don't know how many men Zilar sent. The tavern wench—Dolssa's friend—didn't overhear that detail." He eyed his brother warily. "He might have sent a handful of assassins to *le Château de Tours* to await Ibarra's arrival. Or he might have sent a small army. We won't know until they attack."

"My guess is he sent Gizon—his most trusted man—to kill Ibarra with your blade. And that bear, Urdin. They're probably leading a group of Zilar's henchmen, posing as travelers or merchants. Zilar might even have spies among Ibarra's own men." Gaultier's expression was grim.

"Precisely why we need to separate him from the caravan and get him quickly to the Tower." Xabi signaled the awaiting mounted knights, indicating his readiness to depart. As Cardin and Gaultier climbed into their saddles, he shouted, "Let's move. *Allons-y!*"

****

The winter sun was at its zenith when Cardin spotted Ibarra's entourage winding slowly along the dirt road. Mounted knights displaying the blue-and-gold French flag of King Philippe le Bel led the procession. Outside each of the two ornately carved wooden carriages, four armored knights defended the caravan of royal gifts headed toward Paris. Behind the carriage transporting Comte Ibarra, eight additional knights defended the rear of the noble *cortège.*

Holding the royal French banner to identify themselves, Cardin—accompanied by Gaultier and six knights from *le Château de Montmarin,* with an extra horse for Ibarra to ride—rode up to the front of the procession, which had halted at their approach. Four knights from Biarritz rode up to greet them.

"*Egun on*, Zubiri and Elizondo." Cardin used the friendly Basque greeting to address two of the approaching knights whom he recognized, having served with them for six years at *le Château de Montmarin.* "We must take Comte Ibarra immediately to *la Tour Blanche* for his safety. We need to remove him from the caravan so he can leave with us—we've brought an additional horse for him to ride." Cardin gestured to the saddled Friesian mount whose reins Gaultier held in his left hand. "Andoni Zilar has sent men to assassinate Ibarra, to prevent him from signing the Alliance with Aquitaine treaty. Xabi Vazquez and his men will help you defend the carriages in case you're attacked on the way to the Tower. But Comte Ibarra needs to come with us at once."

Zubiri, astride his gleaming black stallion, exchanged glances as he conferred quickly and silently with his companions. Ducking his chin in agreement, he took the reins of the extra horse from Gaultier's outstretched hand. "I'll fetch Ibarra and return at once. Elizondo and I will ride with you."

Moments later, a harried and distraught Comte Ibarra rode up with Zubiri to join Cardin, Gaultier, and the knights from *Montmarin.*

"Quickly, sir. To *la Tour Blanche!*" Verifying that Ibarra was at his side, and that Gaultier, Zubiri, Elizondo, and the knights were close behind, Cardin galloped off, leading the way to Issoudun.

****

Built by King Richard the Lionheart in the twelfth

century, *la Tour Blanche* was a cylindrical fortress made of pristine white stone with thick, impenetrable walls, arrow slit windows, and a roof equipped with a *hourdage*—a wooden gallery with corbelling and an overhang so that defenders could launch projectiles or pour boiling oil upon attackers. Originally an English fortification of the Plantagênet dynasty, *la Tour Blanche* had reverted to the French crown and was now a royal fortress of King Philippe le Bel.

As the hilltop tower came into sight, Cardin waved the French flag while Gaultier held the banner of *le Château de Montmarin.* The watchtower guards, recognizing the coat of arms of Comte Eztebe Ibarra, staunch ally of their sovereign, King Philippe of France, lowered the drawbridge at the base of the hill to allow entrance across the moat.

The hairs on the back of Cardin's neck rose in sudden alert. As a volley of arrows whizzed by, he flew up the hill, jumped off his horse, and yanked Comte Ibarra from the saddle. Arrows rained down upon them as Cardin whisked Ibarra inside *la Tour Blanche,* handing him over to the guards of Pierre Chalamet, Lord of the White Tower. "Get archers to the parapets. We're under attack!"

Metal screeched as swords clashed behind him. Cardin slammed the tower door shut and spun around to find Gaultier, Zubiri, Elizondo, and their knights engaged in heavy combat. Elizondo had fallen from his horse, blood oozing from his helmet as he battled a mounted knight. An archer from a rooftop parapet of the tower fired three arrows into Elizondo's attacker, halting the enemy sword mid-arc from swooping down for the kill. Gaultier and Zubiri were each fighting two mounted opponents, and several of the knights from Montmarin were surrounded and outnumbered. With the watchtower guard killed, the drawbridge remained open, permitting more attackers to fly across the bridge and enter the fray.

Cardin's longbow and quiver of arrows were still strapped to his horse's saddle. Slashing with his sword, he fought his way across the bloody, mud-strewn courtyard, retrieved his longbow, and fired at the knights approaching the bridge. He slew four, who fell from their horses just outside the entrance gate. As he nocked another arrow, drew his bowstring and took aim, a pummeling force knocked him off his feet and flung him backward. Paralyzed by a searing, burning pain in his chest, Cardin succumbed to a thick, smothering blanket of darkness.

****

A horrorstruck Gaultier saw the crossbow bolt strike his brother in the chest, piercing the chain mail armor with sufficient force to lift him up into the air and knock him flat on his back. Bleeding heavily from the gaping wound, Cardin now lay sprawled across the muck and gore of the contained battlefield in front of *la Tour Blanche*. Yet before he could help his critically injured brother, Gaultier had to eliminate the two enemy knights he was currently battling. With a vicious slash to the upper thigh, he toppled one mounted combatant from his horse, impaling him with the lethal tip of his sword. Whirling around to parry the blow from the other, who had lunged forward to attack, he carried the momentum of his spin into a savage downward slice that disarmed his opponent.

Zubiri, who had slain two knights, beheaded Gaultier's assailant from behind and bellowed to

Elizondo. "Raise the drawbridge!"

Elizondo flew up the stairs into the wooden watchtower gate, cranked the winch, and raised the heavy bridge while Gaultier, Zubiri, and the knights from Montmarin slew the remaining attackers in the courtyard of *la Tour Blanche*.

Gaultier scanned the bloody terrain. Two dozen enemy corpses—many with severed limbs or bodies riddled with arrows from the fortress archers—littered the gruesome battlefield. Several of their own knights had been killed, and some seriously wounded. But none except Cardin had been impaled by a crossbow bolt. Wiping sweat and blood from his injured face, Gaultier yelled to Zubiri, who strode across the courtyard toward him. "Help me get Cardin inside."

Gaultier shouted up to the rooftop archers. "Open the door! We have wounded men!"

A few moments later, the tower guards unbolted the front entrance, permitting Gaultier and Zubiri to carry the critically wounded Cardin inside while other knights brought in the injured men. Lord Chalamet quickly led them to a large stone chamber with a high ceiling, towering walls, and narrow slits for windows. Along one side of the cavernous room, beds were lined up against the massive stone wall.

Flustered and distraught, Comte Ibarra rushed toward them, eyeing the critically wounded Cardin. "I owe him my life. He got me inside the tower." Gratitude and grief warred in his frantic, desperate gaze.

"Lay him here," Chalamet said, indicating an available mattress. "The healer will assess his injury." Dark hair streaked with grey, his thick brows furrowed in concern, the lord of *la Tour Blanche* gestured for an elderly robed man to approach as Gaultier and Zubiri settled an unconscious Cardin onto the straw palette.

The white-haired healer bent over the prone body to examine Cardin's gruesome chest wound. Crusted with drying blood, the wooden shaft of the crossbow bolt protruded several inches from the punctured chain mail armor. "The metal tip of the arrow penetrated the muscle in his chest." When the healer rose to his full stooped height, the grim regard in his bleak eyes confirmed the bitter truth that Gaultier already knew. *Cardin has little chance of survival.* "I dare not remove the bolt, for he will bleed to death very quickly. Yet if the quarrel remains embedded, the wound will fester. And he will die slowly…in agony."

Gaultier gazed mournfully at his brother's pallid face, his heart clenching at the tragic irony. *Basati finally bonded with his abandoned son. The Basque Wolf of Biarritz found love once again. And now—just when he finds happiness after drowning in so much sorrow—his life hangs by a mere thread, I've got to get him back to Brocéliande. To Ulla. She's an exceptional healer. She loves him with all her heart. If anyone can save him, she will.* He raised his bowed head to meet Lord Chalamet's concerned gaze. "Do you have a wagon I could borrow to transport him?"

"Yes, there's a supply wagon you may use. But my archers report more armored knights are fast approaching the Tower. How can you leave when we're still under attack?" Chalamet regarded Gaultier with stunned incredulity.

"We'll get up to the roof. Fire at the enemy. See how many of Zilar's men remain." Gaultier turned away from Chalamet and spoke reassuringly to a still shaken Comte

Ibarra. "Xabi Vazquez and the knights from Montmarin are defending your royal carriages. We sent a message to King Philippe in *le Palais-Royal* several days ago, informing him of the assassination plot and requesting reinforcements to escort you to Paris. With the king's royal guards, we'll ensure that you arrive in time to sign the Yuletide treaty." With a respectful nod to each nobleman, Gaultier retreated from Comte Ibarra and Lord Chalamet. Summoning Zubiri, Elizondo, and the uninjured knights with a swoop of his arm, he raced toward the stairwell at the rear of the room. "*To the parapets*!"

The winding, circular steps led up to the flat rooftop of the one-hundred-foot-tall tower, where archers with longbows defended the fortress between openings of the crenellated embrasure. As Gaultier and his men arrived on the scene, they quickly assumed positions behind the raised merlon sections of the defensive wall where they nocked their arrows and fired down upon the enemy from strategic gaps in the battlements.

From this height above the treetops, Gaultier observed Xabi and the knights of Montmarin battling attackers and defending the two heavily laden carriages from within the protective circle they had formed around the valuable cargo. As he watched his brother's closest friend valiantly defend Comte Ibarra's royal gifts for the King of France, arrows from longbowmen atop the Tower eliminated several of Zilar's mounted henchmen. Gaultier fired several times in rapid succession, but without the extended reach of a superior longbow, his arrows fell far short of their intended marks.

Just as the winter sun began its early evening descent, the thunderous pounding of hooves announced the fortuitous arrival of a bevy of armored knights. Clad in blue surcoats bearing the three golden *fleur-de-lys* emblems of King Philippe le Bel of France, the royal soldiers swiftly and efficiently dispatched the remainder of Andoni Zilar's attackers. Triumphant and glorious, the Parisian knights joined Xabi and his men as the royal procession continued proudly along the cobblestone road toward the entrance to *la Tour Blanche d' Issoudun.*

The defenders of the Tower lowered their longbows and cheered in victory. One of Lord Chalamet's archers hollered down to the watchtower guard, "Lower the drawbridge!"

His scarred, sweaty face aglow in the golden light, Zubiri grinned from ear to ear as the royal French guards led the cavalcade of knights and two carriages across the moat and into the courtyard in front of the Tower. "Let's go congratulate Xabi. This calls for a celebration!" As if suddenly remembering Cardin's grievous injury, Zubiri's jubilant expression became grim. "You must leave at once. Even a brief delay could mean the difference between life and death for your brother."

Gaultier nodded solemnly as Elizondo walked up to join them. "I'll take my father's knights and depart tonight for *le Château de Landuc*. Cardin's—Basati's—betrothed is a gifted healer. So is our mother. I pray the two of them can cure my brother."

"*Zorte on*. Good luck. I hope they can save Basati." Empathy exuding from his seasoned warrior gaze, Zubiri gripped Gaultier's shoulders in an encouraging fraternal embrace. "Come. Let's go downstairs and greet Xabi. We'll help you load your brother into the carriage for the trip home."

Gaultier, Zubiri, Elizondo, and the fortress archers

descended the spiraling stairs to a raucous commotion in the wide entry foyer. Knights filed into the Tower through the enormous entrance door, crossing the antechamber into the large ceremonial hall, *la Salle d'Honneur.* Harried servants ushered the injured to available beds, bandaging wounds and offering mugs of ale along the wall where a still unconscious Cardin lay upon a straw pallet. Outside the entrance door, Gaultier glimpsed stable hands leading the horse-drawn royal carriages from the drawbridge into the safety of the inner courtyard. Tower guards and knights retrieved the bodies of their fallen, strapped atop riderless horses, gathering lifeless victims strewn across the bloodstained courtyard in preparation for honorable burial. Enemy corpses were unceremoniously tossed into a heap for subsequent burning.

Xabi dismounted from his horse, handed the reins to a stable hand, and headed toward Gaultier, his bearded face beaming with triumph. "The royal guards arrived just in time. I didn't know how much longer we would last." He shook hands with Zubiri and Elizondo, accepting their congratulatory enthusiasm, all the while scanning the perimeter of the entry foyer, obviously looking for his closest friend. "Where's Basati?"

Gaultier indicated *la Salle d' Honneur* with a toss of his head. "In here." He led Xabi through the high, arched entryway into the cavernous chamber where two roaring fires blazed in stone hearths and the pitiful moans of the wounded pierced the wintry air. When they arrived at Cardin's bedside, Xabi groaned and dropped to one knee. "He was hit by a crossbow bolt. The healer can't remove it—he lacks the skill to perform the necessary surgery. I have to get him back to Brocéliande. His betrothed Ulla is a *guérisseuse*—a gifted Priestess of Dana, like my mother. I must leave tonight."

Lord Chalamet, who had been directing attendants to serve food and drinks to the uninjured, crossed the ceremonial hall and approached Cardin's bed as Xabi rose to his feet. Chalamet's deep, calm voice conveyed compassion and concern as he addressed Gaultier. "My men are harnessing the horses and loading supplies into the wagon. It will be ready for your departure in half an hour." From the thick folds of his black velvet robe, he extended a welcoming arm and gestured toward a trestle table near the inviting warmth of the fireplace. "You must eat a hearty meal before you leave. It will sustain you on your journey." He smiled graciously as Comte Ibarra and the captain of the royal Parisian guards joined their small group.

"My lord," Xabi said, lowering his head respectfully to address Comte Ibarra. "My men and I rode hard from Biarritz to intercept you en route before you reached *le Château de Tours*, where Zilar planned your assassination. When flooding forced you east to *la Tour Blanche*, we knew his men would attack you here—to stop you from reaching Paris and signing the Yuletide treaty." Xabi scanned the famished knights at the tables in *la Salle d' Honneur* who were devouring platters of cold meats and imbibing mugs of ale. "Which one of your men is named Uribe? He's an English spy, loyal to Edward Longshanks. He was ordered to allow Zilar's assassin to enter your private chambers to commit the crime." Xabi removed a knife from the sheath at his waist and displayed the unique, ornately carved wolf head dagger with the dazzling emerald eye. "With this weapon—*Basati's blade.*" He indicated the critically injured Cardin with a nod of his head. "You were right," he said as he handed the knife to Gaultier. "Zilar sent Gizon to commit the crime. By using this wolf head dagger, they knew Basati would take the blame. Zilar would stop the Alliance with Aquitaine and be appointed the new Lord of Montmarin."

A stunned Ibarra responded to Xabi's question. "That man is Uribe," he said, indicating one of his own knights with a long nose and pointed beard. He turned toward Lord Chalamet. "Is there a prison here in the Tower?"

Chalamet nodded. "Underground. We store supplies in the cellar, on the first level below. But beneath that, we have a holding cell for prisoners. You can lock him up there."

Ibarra addressed the captain of the royal Parisian guards standing at his side. "Arrest Uribe. Take him underground to the prison cell. We'll bring him with us when we leave for Paris in the morning. King Philippe will decide his fate."

The blond-haired captain's blue eyes blazed in the firelight. "The Iron King has no tolerance for treason. Uribe will be executed as an English spy."

Gaultier watched as the captain of the royal guards summoned four of his fellow knights. Together, they stormed across *la Salle d' Honneur*, seized the seated Uribe, and hauled him to his feet. While two guards pinned him in place with the tips of their swords pointed at his neck, two others shackled his wrists with manacles and chains. Dragging the prisoner from the ceremonial hall toward the stairwell at the back of the room, they descended the steps leading underground and disappeared from view.

"Tomorrow, at first light, we'll bury our fallen and burn the bodies of the enemy. The knights of Montmarin will join the Parisian guards in escorting you safely to Paris, my lord. We'll join your entourage and accompany you back to Biarritz after the signing of the Yuletide treaty." Zuribi removed his chain mail coif and bowed his head respectfully to Comte Ibarra.

"Excellent. Now please allow me to offer you my hospitality. Come, enjoy a hearty meal as my honored guests." Lord Chalamet proudly led their group to his own private table upon a raised dais, summoning attentive servants with a gesture of his commanding hand.

While Xabi, Elizondo, and Zuribi eagerly dug into the salted roast boar, tangy ripe cheese, and thick hearty bread, Gaultier forced down the tasteless food, anxious to be on the road home to Brocéliande. He closed his eyes and silently prayed for his grievously wounded brother. *Please let Cardin survive the journey. And please let Ulla heal him.*

"Once we deliver Comte Ibarrra to Paris and the Yuletide treaty is signed, I'll ride to Brocéliande with your brother Bastien and King Guillemin of Finistère to join you at *le Château de Landuc*." A glimmer of hope flickered amidst the grief in Xabi's dark eyes. "For Basati's Twelfth Night wedding." He raised his goblet, prompting Gaultier to do the same. "To Ulla. May she heal his body as she did his broken heart."

His throat clenching, Gaultier swallowed his sorrow with a great gulp of ale.

Lord Chalamet, having seated and served his guests, returned to Gaultier's side. "I'm providing torches to light your way. You can cover fifty miles tonight before you must stop to rest the horses. At that rate, you'll reach Brocéliande in three or four days."

While Gaultier finished the salted boar and drained his mug of ale, two Tower guards approached Lord Chalamet and reported that the wagon to transport Cardin was loaded and ready.

Gaultier rose to his feet, wiping froth from his mouth with the sleeve of his tunic. He nodded to Padrig, one of his father's most trusted knights and the leader of the group who would accompany him back to *le Château de Landuc*. "Have the men saddle the horses and prepare to depart. I'll get my brother settled into the wagon."

Padrig rounded up the knights from Landuc, who hastily finished their meal, rose from the table, and filed out the front door of *la Tour Blanche.*

Comte Ibarra and Lord Chalamet accompanied Gaultier and Xabi into the *Salle d' Honneur* where a still unconscious Cardin lay on his straw pallet. Two of Lord Chalamet's men stood beside the bed, holding a wooden stretcher.

"Use this to carry him out to the wagon. Secure him with blankets and ropes to keep him stable during the voyage." Chalamet nodded to his two men. "My guards will assist you."

The white-haired healer approached Gaultier as they settled Cardin onto the litter. "He was restless about an hour ago and drank a few swallows of water. If he regains consciousness again, have him drink as much as possible. Good luck. I pray your healer has more skill than I."

Two dozen mounted knights from *le Château de Landuc* awaited Gaultier in front of the Tower as he and Xabi carried the stretcher across the bloodstained courtyard, past the pile of enemy corpses and the bodies of their own fallen knights. Xabi and Lord Chalamet's two guards helped him settle Cardin's stretcher in the back of the wagon among the supplies for the four-day journey.

Dark eyes glimmering in the flickering torchlight, white teeth gleaming in his thick, bushy beard, Xabi gripped Gaultier's arms in a tight, fraternal embrace. "Travel safely to Brocéliande. I'll join you at *le Château de Landuc* before the Winter Solstice. I plan on being the best man at Basati's Twelfth Night wedding."

Gaultier bid farewell to Comte Ibarra, Lord Chalamet, and the royal Parisian guards. He waved goodbye to Xabi, Zubiri, Elizondo, and the knights of Montmarin. Mounting his magnificent Friesian stallion, he rode in front of the wagon transporting his wounded brother. And, with a nod to the two drivers and the commanding knight Padrig, he set off in the cold, black winter night for the Forest of Brocéliande.

Chapter 19

Winter Solstice

The warm, spicy aroma of cinnamon mingled with the clean scent of pine as Ulla helped Laudine wrap evergreen garlands around the supportive pillars in the expansive Great Hall of *le Château de Landuc*. Above the two enormous hearths where crackling fires warmed the vast chamber against the mid-December chill, evergreen boughs with pinecones, berries, and fragrant cloves added to the festive ambiance. With the help of cheerful servants, the two women were finishing the castle decorations in preparation for the Yuletide holidays, which would begin with the Winter Solstice celebration and Lukaz' birthday, and culminate with the glorious Twelfth Night wedding on Three Kings' Day, *la Fête des Rois*.

Laudine's daughter-in-law Gabrielle had arrived several days ago with her royal entourage from Finistère, bringing her four children to *le Château de Landuc* to spend the holiday season with their grandparents. Soon, Gabrielle's husband Bastien and father King Guilllemin would be arriving to celebrate Lukaz' birthday—and Gabrielle and Bastien's wedding anniversary—on the Winter Solstice.

Ulla's sumptuous red velvet wedding gown was

complete, the tailor had finished Cardin's magnificent gold velvet tunic and black woolen breeches, and the village goldsmith had properly sized the two wedding rings. Everything was ready for the glorious Twelfth Night wedding.

But Ulla could not shake the foreboding premonition that something was terribly wrong. Cardin needed her. She could feel it in her very bones.

"*En garde!*" The voice of ten-year-old Gunnar reverberated through the cavernous Great Hall as he engaged his younger brother Haldar in a mock battle with wooden swords and shields.

"All knights must train outside in the lists, not inside the castle." Gabrielle—who had joined Laudine and Ulla in decorating the Great Hall—laid down the white hellebore blossoms she was tucking into a holiday wreath and shooed her two oldest sons toward the imposing front entrance door.

"I'm going to be a castle archer, like my father." Lukaz nocked a fletched arrow, tautly drawing back the string of his finely crafted bow, as if to demonstrate his already impressive skills.

Curiosity evident on their intrigued young faces, Gunnar and Haldar stopped in the doorway and turned to watch Lukaz exhibit his fine form.

"My papa is the Basati, the Basque Wolf of Biarritz. But he's not going back to Aquitaine. He's staying here in Bretagne. With me. And bringing me with him to *le Château de Beaufort* after he marries Lady Ulla." Expressive blue eyes widened with pride, he grinned triumphantly at his older cousins. "My father is Sir Cardin de Landuc. Captain of the Royal Archers for King Guillemin of Finistère. When he marries Lady Ulla, the three of us will be a family, and we will live together at *le Château de Beaufort.*" He lifted his chin in exultant defiance. *"*I'm not a bastard anymore.*"*

Gabrielle smiled lovingly at the future castle archer, the nephew whom she and Bastien had raised since birth. "That's right," she agreed, encouraging Lukaz to lower his drawn arrow with a gesture of her hand. "Your papa will teach you to become a castle archer, just like him. You'll live with us in Finistère—and train to become a knight with Gunnar and Haldar." She glanced sternly at her two oldest sons, conveying her expectation that they would accept Lukaz and treat him fairly. "When Vidar is old enough in a few years, he'll join the three of you, too. We'll all be a big, happy family." She beamed at Laudine and Ulla, who had paused their holiday decorating to observe the cousins' chivalrous display. "And every Yuletide season, we'll come here to visit *Mamie* and *Papi* at *le Château de Landuc.*" Ushering the three whooping, jubilant boys outside into the afternoon light of the setting sun, Gabrielle announced, "Practice now, while you still have enough daylight. It will soon be time for supper."

As the knights-in-training stormed out of the castle, shouting with glee, the flame-haired French princess lifted her wailing infant daughter from the cradle on the floor and settled down to nurse her in a tufted chair near the crackling hearth. "I am delighted that Cardin has acknowledged his son," she said to Laudine and Ulla as they resumed wrapping evergreen garlands around a supportive pillar. "It was so hard for Lukaz to be ridiculed and humiliated as a bastard. Now that his father has returned, no one will ever call him that again." Gabrielle kissed her babe's soft auburn curls and looked up at Ulla. Maternal lovelight glowed in her generous eyes. "After the wedding—you'll be the *Maman* Lukaz never had. Reunited with his papa, a mother to love him at long last…he'll have a true family. The greatest Yuletide gift he could ever receive."

Ulla's eyes brimmed with joyful tears. She loved Lukaz with all her heart and wanted desperately to become his *Maman*. As she watched Gabrielle nurse her infant daughter, her own breasts tingled at the thought of Cardin's child now thriving in her womb. She couldn't wait to tell him the wonderful news. If only she could shake the horrid anxiety that plagued her. Wiping damp palms against her woolen gown, she smiled gratefully at Gabrielle's generous praise.

The thunderous pounding of horses' hooves in the courtyard sent several servants scurrying to greet the unexpected visitors. Her face alight with anticipation and delight, Laudine dropped the evergreen garland she was holding and rushed toward the door. "Gaultier and Cardin have returned!"

Ulla's heart hammered in her chest. Although Laudine was thrilled that her sons had returned, Ulla knew intuitively that something was dreadfully wrong.

And that Cardin desperately needed her.

Swallowing the bile that rose to her constricted throat, she ran to the front door.

And nearly swooned at the sight of Gaultier, Padrig, and two other knights transporting a bloodied, grotesquely wounded Cardin strapped onto a wooden stretcher.

"Bring him in here," Laudine shouted as the men entered the castle, indicating a small bedroom near the kitchen alcove where Maëlys sometimes slept. "Lay him on the bed. What happened?" Her voice quavering, she hovered over her injured son, assessing the grievous puncture wound where a bloodied arrow protruded from the pierced chain mail armor. She straightened and spun to Gaultier, her stricken face crumpled in grief.

"Zilar's men attacked us just as we reached Issoudun. Cardin got Comte Ibarra safely inside the Tower, but took a crossbow bolt in the chest. The healer at *la Tour Blanche* didn't have sufficient skill to remove the arrow, so I rushed him home to you and Ulla. Can you save him?" Gaultier's deep voice cracked as Esclados, Lukaz, and Quentin rushed into the room.

"Papa!" Lukaz shrieked, rushing to his unconscious father's side. Tears streamed down his ruddy cheeks, flushed from the cold winter chill of training as knights with his cousins in the lists.

Limbs shaking with horror, Ulla stared in stunned disbelief at Cardin's ravaged body. As she hugged Lukaz tight, vainly trying to comfort the sobbing little boy she loved so very much, her instincts as a healer took over, spurring her to act. Handing Lukaz gently over to his grandmother, she conveyed the silent message to Laudine with imploring, desperate eyes. *Take him. I'll rush home, get my supplies, and be right back.*

Weaving frantically through the throng of men crowded around Cardin's bed, Ulla dashed from the room and raced out the back door of the castle kitchen.

Vill—who had been lying on the floor near the back door—sensed her urgency, leapt to his feet, and bounded with her toward the forest, sprinting across the snow-dusted courtyard.

Ulla bolted up the front steps of her stone cottage, clumsily unlocked the wooden entrance door, and raced into the kitchen to retrieve her satchel of herbs from the corner cupboard. *I'll need healing crystals, too. Amber and carnelian to strengthen his stamina. Celestite and opal to fight disease. Emerald to bathe him in the verdant healing power of the forest. And curative waters from the sacred spring.* Tucking the selected gemstones into a protective pouch within her leather bag, she hoisted it over her shoulder and grabbed an earthenware container to fill at the well.

Dashing out the front door, she ran through the dense woods, stopping at the Fountain of Barenton—the sacred spring in the heart of the Forest of Brocéliande. Kneeling beside the gurgling underground spring, she filled the ceramic jug to the brim and closed it with a cork stopper. Whistling for Vill, she raced through the forest, bringing the sacred water, curative herbs, and healing crystals back into the castle.

****

Inside the quiet, vacant chamber where a now naked Cardin lay upon a linen-covered straw mattress, the cleansing aroma of burning sage purified the still air. A blazing fire crackled in the stone hearth and warmed the small room against December's winter chill. Laudine stood near a marble-topped walnut sideboard upon which she had assembled a variety of herbs, tinctures, and ointments to treat her critically wounded son. On the table near the lone window, a sweet-smelling beeswax candle glowed in the golden light of the setting sun.

"Lukaz is with Gaultier, Esclados, and Quentin. I asked them to take him riding and keep him occupied while we remove the arrow. I took off Cardin's blood-soaked armor and cleansed his wound with calendula soap and yarrow leaf." Laudine walked over to stand beside her son's bed, taking hold of Ulla's shaking hands and fixing her with a determined, encouraging stare. Wisdom sparkled in her amber eyes. "We will save him, you and I. With our divine healing skills as Priestesses of Dana and with the overwhelming love we both have for him in our hearts." She hugged Ulla tight, then released her, gesturing to a knife upon the walnut sideboard. "Place the tip of the dagger in the flame. The fire will purify the blade."

Ulla complied, handing the heated instrument to Laudine. Legs quivering under her woolen gown, she examined the gruesome gash in Cardin's lower left shoulder. Around the puncture wound where the wooden arrow shaft protruded, his decaying flesh was swollen and inflamed, oozing a noxious, foul-smelling fluid. *A few inches lower, and it would have pierced his heart. Dear Goddess, please help us save him. I pray that we are not too late.*

"I will make an incision here," Laudine explained, indicating an area to the left of the wound. "When I pull back the skin, use the tweezers to grasp the quarrel and carefully remove the arrowhead." With the razor-sharp blade, she meticulously sliced into the skin of Cardin's upper chest, causing a sudden surge of bright red blood.

Ulla wiped the flow with a clean cloth, gripped the metal arrowhead with tweezers, and carefully withdrew the embedded crossbow bolt. While Laudine examined the incision to make sure no fragments of metal remained in Cardin's flesh, Ulla laid the long wooden shaft with its bloodstained tip upon the sideboard table.

With Laudine's knife, Ulla painstakingly cut away a small area of diseased skin around Cardin's wound. She wiped the blade clean, returned it to Laudine, and crossed the room to retrieve a small kettle from the hearth. Pouring hot water into a cup on the table, she stirred in a mixture of crushed raw garlic, sage, rosemary, and calendula. Cautioning Laudine to step back, Ulla trickled the scalding concoction into Cardin's open wound, setting the empty cup aside and stanching the new bleeding with a poultice of yarrow.

"Your sewing skills are much finer than mine." Laudine handed Ulla a needle and thread.

Soaking the instruments in a bowl of wine, Ulla meticulously cleansed all debris from Cardin's wound and closed the incision with precisely detailed stitches. She cut off the excess thread with Laudine's knife, wiped the needle clean, and placed it back inside her satchel. With a soft cloth, a bucket of water, and sweet-smelling calendula soap, she washed the blood and gore from the dark hair stretched across Cardin's chest. Applying a healing ointment of garlic and honey over the row of neat stitches, she bandaged the wound with soft, pure white linen.

Ulla lovingly washed every inch of Cardin's blood-soaked body and filthy hair, whispering silent prayers that her nurturing care would save him. While Laudine carefully lifted Cardin's shoulder, Ulla removed the soiled bed sheet from beneath him, replacing it with a fresh one and covering him with woolen blankets. Retrieving the gemstones from the pouch in her satchel, she placed five crystals—one at his head and at each of his four limbs—forming a star to channel the divine healing energy of the Goddess into Cardin's damaged body. Eyes closed in fervent concentration, she drew upon the curative powers of the crystals, willing the man she loved so desperately to live.

Laudine wrapped the bloodied linens into a ball and handed them to a servant for proper cleaning. She returned to Ulla's side and draped an arm across her back, giving her shoulders a comforting squeeze. "Stay here and rest." She pulled a velvet tufted chair up to Cardin's bedside and sat Ulla down, kissing her firmly on the cheek. "I'll take care of Lukaz and assist Maëlys with supper. I'll bring him in later to see his papa and say goodnight. And I'll have Jehan set up a bed in here for you—and bring a platter of food as well. You must keep up your strength." Laudine brushed a lock of long black hair from Ulla's weary face. "We've done all we can for now. If he awakens, have him drink the water from the sacred well." She headed toward the door, turning back at the threshold. "You're the most gifted healer I've ever known. If anyone can save Cardin, it's you. I pray you will, Ulla. For all of us." Tears glimmering in her golden eyes, Laudine smiled bravely and left the room, closing the heavy wooden door behind her.

Ulla rose from her chair, crossed the room, and retrieved her satchel. *I'll mix healing herbs into the water from the sacred spring. Calendula to withdraw poison from the wound. Burdock root and red clover to cleanse his blood. Goosegrass to reduce the swelling and inflammation.* From the ceramic jug she'd carried into the castle, Ulla poured water into a goblet on Cardin's bedside table, mixing in carefully measured droplets of each tincture. *I hope he stirs soon, so I can coax him to drink. Please, dear Goddess, help me save him.*

She must have dozed off in the chair, for she was startled awake by deep, anguished moaning. Cardin was burning with fever, thrashing restlessly in bed. Ulla calmed him with a soothing touch, planting soft kisses

179

on his hot cheeks as she stroked his damp hair. Lifting his head, she held the goblet to his lips, helping him gulp a few swallows of herb-laced water. When he settled back down to sleep, she put a cool compress on his forehead and changed his bandage, adding more crushed garlic and raw honey to the stitches over his wound. She replaced the curative crystals at the five astral points around his body, replenishing the divine energy of the star with fresh healing gemstones.

Pouring some of the liquid from the ceramic jug into a small bowl, Ulla cleansed the used crystals in the purifying water of the sacred spring. Tomorrow, she would replace the five gemstones at each astral point around Cardin's body once again, bathing him anew in refreshed healing energy.

As promised, Jehan set up a pallet for her along the wall near Cardin's bed. A short while later, Maëlys popped in with an appealing platter of venison pottage and winter vegetables from Laudine's *verrière,* half a loaf of crusty fresh bread, a wedge of ripe cheese, and a pewter goblet of ale. "Healers must eat," she admonished affectionately, setting the tray down upon the walnut sideboard. Worry creased her forehead as she glanced at the sleeping Cardin. "Any change?"

Ulla shook her head and lowered her eyes. Her stomach grumbled at the enticing aroma of the appetizing food. Indicating the platter with a gesture of her hand, she ducked her chin in gratitude and sat down to eat.

"Laudine will be in soon with Lukaz. He keeps asking about his father. I hope, for his sake, that Cardin improves." Maëlys smiled politely and nodded at the tray. "I'll be back later to collect the dishes. Eat as much as you can…to keep up your strength." With a respectful bow, the irreplaceable servant and indispensable cook discreetly disappeared.

Ulla ate all of the delicious pottage, savoring the rich broth, flavorful herbs, and hearty oats. She spread creamy cheese over the crusty bread, popping the last bite into her mouth when Laudine and Lukaz appeared in the doorway.

"Is Papa going to live? That's all I want for my birthday." Lukaz crossed the room and rested his small hand on his father's thick forearm. Expressive eyes widened with fear, he looked imploring at Ulla. "It's my Yuletide wish, too. All I want for Christmas is for Papa to live."

As Ulla rose to her feet, Lukaz flung his arms around her waist, sobbing into her woolen gown. "Please heal him—just like you did Vill. Please, Lady Ulla. Heal Papa."

She stroked the soft waves of his dark hair, rocking him against her stomach. *I wish I could soothe him with comforting words. I long for the voice I once had.*

"Ulla and I will do everything we can to save your Papa. But he needs to sleep, and so do you. Now, kiss him goodnight. And say *bonne nuit* to Lady Ulla." Laudine waited while Lukaz complied. As she led her sniffling grandson off to bed, she added cheerfully, "Come, I'll tell you the tale of how Sir Tristan of Lyonesse became the Dragon Knight of Avalon."

****

The next three days passed in a dull haze. Cardin occasionally roused enough to swallow a few gulps of the herb-infused water, but he did not fully regain consciousness. Servants helped Ulla change his urine-soaked bedding, bringing clean linens for bathing and bandages. She repeatedly applied scalding compresses to the festering wound, extracting the poison from the inflamed flesh, coating the injured skin with crushed garlic, calendula, and raw honey. Each morning, she replaced the five purified crystals at his head, arms, and legs, wordlessly invoking the healing essence of the minerals to restore his weakened body. She placed droplets of coriander tincture under his tongue, praying that the rare herb imported from the Mediterranean would reduce his resistant fever and help him awaken from his seemingly endless sleep.

Although Laudine brought Lukaz to visit his papa each morning and night, she insisted that he practice swordsmanship and archery with his cousins and uncles, and continue riding palfreys with his grandfather and Lord Quentin in the afternoon.

Bastien and Xabi arrived on the nineteenth of December with King Guillemin and his royal entourage from Finistère. Jubilant over the successful signing of the Yuletide treaty and the establishment of the Alliance with Aquitaine between Comte Eztebe Ibarra of Biarritz, King Philippe of Paris, and King Guillemin of Finstère, their gaiety was subdued by the critically injured knight who still valiantly battled for his life.

Laudine had just finished helping Ulla change Cardin's bandages and now sat with her at a small table near his bedside, discussing the upcoming Yuletide events. "Today is the Winter Solstice. We need to celebrate Lukaz' birthday as planned. I hope to brighten the holidays as much as possible. And keep the faith that Cardin will recover." Darting a glance at her sleeping son, she poured two cups of chamomile *tisane* and handed one to Ulla. "Maëlys is preparing the wassail—that spicy mulled wine we always drink during the holiday season. Tonight, in keeping with the tradition of our Breton ancestors, I'll bring our guests outside to decorate the large fir tree at the edge of the forest." She pensively sipped her cup of herbal tea. "The castle servants have made plenty of sun-, moon-, and star-shaped ornaments from gold and silver threaded cloth. Lukaz, Gunnar, and Haldar will love hanging the shiny trinkets on the tree. When we come back inside, perhaps you can join us in the solar when Lukaz opens his gifts." Laudine set her cup down and smiled sadly. "I hope he likes the emblem on the new shield Cardin had crafted for him. He wanted Lukaz to bear it proudly—as a future knight of Finistère."

Ulla's heart sank at the dim prospect of Cardin's recovery and the likelihood that Lukaz would return to Finistère without her. She would be alone once again in her small stone cottage, retreating back to the solace of silence.

If Cardin does not survive, I won't be able to keep Lukaz. Or have him live in the cottage with Vill and me. Gabrielle and Bastien will want to take him back to Beaufort. To train him to become a royal knight. A castle archer, like his papa. I can't bear the thought of losing them both. My unborn child will have neither father nor brother. Please, dear Goddess, help me save Cardin. Help me heal the man I love.

As much as she wanted to accept Laudine's invitation to join the celebration in the solar tonight, Ulla refused to leave Cardin's side. His soul was bound to hers, tethered by a delicate lifeline. If she left him, he would die. How could she explain? Ulla had no words.

She scribbled a message on her tablet and handed it to Laudine.

I must stay with Cardin, but I have a gift for Lukaz, too. Please ask Gaultier to fetch it for me. It's on the top shelf in the corner cupboard of my kitchen. Wrapped in silver cloth with a dark green ribbon.

"Of course. I'll have him bring it to you in here. Tonight, after dinner—before we go outside to decorate the tree—Lukaz will come to you so you can give him his gift and celebrate his birthday, too." Laudine finished her *tisane* and rose to her feet, reaching her arms overhead to stretch out her back. "And now, you must excuse me. I need to tend to my royal guests—even if they are my own son and daughter-in-law." She chuckled, bending down to kiss Ulla's two cheeks with *la bise* of farewell. Placing the empty cups beside the teapot, she lifted the metal tray and slipped quietly out the door.

Later, as Ulla mopped sweat from Cardin's fevered brow, Gaultier brought the birthday gift for her to give Lukaz. He laid the cloth-wrapped package on the table and bent down to kiss her cheek. "He still hasn't awakened?" Despair dimmed his bright eyes.

Ulla shook her head softly, unable to hold his sorrowful gaze.

"He will. I have faith that you can save him, Ulla." Gaultier raised her hand to his lips and kissed it softly. "Please heal my brother." With a reverent bow of his dark head, Gaultier retreated from the room.

When Cardin moaned and stirred, Ulla helped him drink more herb-infused water from the sacred spring. She replaced the healing crystals in the five astral points around his head and limbs, and washed his entire body with purifying water from the well. Holding her hand over his inflamed wound, she silently summoned the healing essence of the gemstones and the curative cleansing of the sacred spring.

Dear Goddess Dana, hear my prayer. May your divine spirit pass through these sacred elements of water, forest, and stone that I imbue into Cardin's ravaged body. Guide me—your devout priestess—to heal the man I love. Please make Lukaz' Yuletide wish come true.

Night fell, and the still room became dark. Ulla lit a beeswax candle, added a log to the fire, and returned to sit beside the bed. She held Cardin's hand, absently rubbing the dark hair on his knuckles as she gazed into the flickering flames in the hearth. Seven years ago, Cardin sat beside his beloved wife as she labored to give birth to his son.

A jubilant Lukaz burst into the room, his effervescence and enthusiasm instantly squelched at the sight of his stricken father. "I wanted to show you my shield," he said apologetically, displaying the gift Cardin had requisitioned from the local armorer for his son's birthday. Across the top of the kite-shaped wooden shield, five black ermine symbols—emblems of *la Bretagne*—stood on a white background above the golden-horned ram and rearing lion, the royal heraldry of Finistère.

Ulla gracefully accepted the fine weapon as Lukaz handed it to her with honor blazing in his bright blue eyes. She nodded in approval as her fingers caressed the smooth, polished wood, admiring the intricate details and superb craftsmanship. With an appreciative smile, she returned the tapered shield to its proud new owner.

"It's perfect for a future knight of Finistère." Laudine stroked the dark, shiny waves of Lukaz' thick hair that so resembled his father's. "When your papa awakens, he'll be delighted to see how much his gift pleases you." She smiled bravely as she met Ulla's gaze. "Lady Ulla has a birthday gift for you, too. She asked me to bring you here so she could give it to you."

Ulla rose to her feet and left Cardin's side. She strode across the room to the walnut sideboard where the wrapped gift sat upon the marble tabletop. The silver threads in the finely woven cloth sparkled in the firelight. She handed the gift to Lukaz and watched as he opened her handmade gift.

"A new falconry glove!" he exclaimed with glee, sliding his hand into the brown deerskin lined with soft rabbit fur. "I can wear it when we hunt with Rask and Finn!"

You can bring Rask with you back to le Château de Beaufort. And wear your new glove in Finistère. Ulla swallowed an enormous lump of sorrow at the thought of losing the little boy whom she already loved like a son. How could she ever let him go? But if Cardin did not survive, she would have no claim to Lukaz. He would go back to Beaufort without her.

Laudine slid an appreciative fingertip over the straps of the falconry glove. "It's adjustable—to accommodate your growth as you become a seasoned hunter." She hugged Lukaz to her ample maternal bosom. "Give Lady Ulla a kiss and thank her for the wonderful gift."

While Lukaz hugged Ulla, expressing his gratitude as he fervently kissed her cheek, Laudine announced, "It's time to join our guests and decorate the Yuletide tree. It's a Breton tradition for the Winter Solstice that dates back to our Celtic ancestors." She smiled at her grandson. "We'll come back to say goodnight to Lady Ulla and your papa after the decorating. Come, let's go join your cousins." Preparing to leave, Laudine bent to kiss Cardin's forehead, whispering words of prayer and encouragement into his unhearing ear. With *la bise* of farewell on Ulla's cheek, she led an exuberant Lukaz from the darkened room.

A clattering of dishes alerted Ulla to someone approaching in the hall. Ruddy cheeks aglow above his blond beard, a beaming Jehan entered the chamber with a platter of sumptuous food. "Since you couldn't join the birthday celebration, milady, I've brought the feast to you." He set a tantalizing tray on the marble-topped walnut sideboard. Ulla glimpsed roast pheasant, baked trout, steaming vegetables from Laudine's greenhouse, and a mouth-watering assortment of sweetmeats that Maëlys must have spent days concocting. "*Bon appétit. Madame.* Enjoy your meal. I'll be back later to fetch the tray." Jehan bowed at the waist and disappeared out the door.

Although the cuisine was superb, Ulla found it difficult to eat. Worry and grief consumed her. At the thought of her unborn child, she forced some of the tasteless food down her constricted throat. *The babe in my womb needs nourishment. And I must stay strong to heal Cardin.*

When she'd eaten enough, she left the tray on the sideboard and returned to the chair at Cardin's side. In the still, dark room, Ulla gazed at the dancing flames in the hearth, her thoughts returning to the night Lukaz was born.

The Winter Solstice. The longest night of the year,

when darkness overwhelms the light. Like now. I sit here in the darkness of despair, losing the man I love, just as Cardin lost Charlotte seven years ago.

Horrific images from the past inundated her in a drowning flood of pain.

Her husband Romain, valiantly but vainly defending their home from murderous, marauding pirates, his throat slashed as he shouted to warn her of the attack.

Her infant son Fjall, slaughtered before her very eyes in his aging nurse's arms.

Her two knights, desperate to save their *châtelaine*, preventing her from leaving the woods where she gathered herbs. Forcing her into the saddle instead. Returning her to Laudine and *le Château de Landuc*. To the Forest of Brocéliande.

I've already lost everyone I love. I cannot lose Cardin, too. Please, dear Goddess, show me how to save him. What more can I do? I've coaxed him to drink water from the sacred spring, laced with herbs from the verdant forest. I've anointed his body with ointments and oils. Surrounded him with healing crystals in the shape of a celestial star. How can I reach him in the darkness? How can I call him back into the light?

As Jehan entered the room to retrieve the tray, Ulla was struck by a flash of inspiration. She leapt to her feet and grasped the servant's sinewy forearm, willing him to stay with imploring eyes. She quickly scribbled a message on her tablet and handed it to him, her pulse pounding in her dry throat.

"I'm sorry, but I cannot read, milady." Bewilderment and shame reflected in his expressive eyes.

Ulla wiped the slate clean and drew an image

instead. When she handed him the tablet, his bearded face stretched into a bemused, astonished grin. "You'd like me to fetch your harp? The one you used to play for us when you were a girl?"

Knees weak and wobbly, she nodded in a fervent frenzy.

"I'll bring it to you, Lady Ulla. Wait here. I'll be right back."

****

Flames scorched his sizzling skin. A raging thirst parched his dry throat. Fire radiated from his chest, his entire body immobilized by incapacitating pain. As darkness and oblivion beckoned, Cardin heard brilliant, glittering strands of ethereal music, drawing him toward a golden light.

The melodic liquid flowed over him like the cascade of a cool, clear spring. Lucid and pure, the limpid notes splashed into a pool of memories, bubbling to the surface.

Pine-scented evergreen boughs with garlands of holly and ivy. Family and friends feasting in the festive Great Hall. Dancing *la carole* to the lively tune of fiddles and flutes. A glorious golden harp bathing the castle in luxurious, luminous sound.

As the melody tugged at his memory, a crystalline voice called to him.

With a song recognized by his soul.

She used to play the harp every holiday season and fill the whole castle with ephemeral, transcendent music. She'd sing the Celtic Yuletide Carol.

The song her heart sings to me now.

Ulla.

She's calling me.

Darkness beckoned. It would be so easy to succumb. To surrender to the numbness. Escape the burning, torturous pain.

The uplifting music rose in volume, a crescendo of sound surging over him like a tumultuous wave crashing against a craggy cliff.

Clear as a clarion bell, the peals of Ulla's angelic voice summoned his soul.

She's calling me. I must find the way back to her.

****

Tears streamed down Ulla's cheeks as she poured herself into her song. With her familiar fingers strumming the silken strings, the music soared like the graceful wings of a swan. From the depths of her soul, she found her voice and called Cardin to come toward the light.

A clamor in the entryway announced the return of the castle guests.

Focused only on reaching Cardin, Ulla continued to strum and sing, her healing essence flowing into his with music, light, and love.

Amid gasps of astonishment, faces appeared in the doorway and family floated into the room.

"Ulla's singing! And playing her harp!" Whispers of wonder rippled like a soft wind.

"That's the Celtic Yuletide Carol she used to always sing. It was your papa's favorite song. Perhaps he'll hear her voice and come back to her." Laudine hugged Lukaz tight. *Please, dear Goddess, help her reach him. Let her heal him with her music and her love.*

As if her prayers had been answered, Cardin opened his eyes.

Ulla stopped playing and handed her harp to

Gaultier, standing at her side. She rose from her chair, and fell to her knees, wiping Cardin's sweaty brow with the palm of her hand. "You came back to me." She kissed his parched lips softly, her tears dampening his bristled cheeks. Supporting his head, she helped him drink more of the herb-infused water from the sacred spring.

A crooked smile of incredulity stretched across his scarred, stubbled face. "I heard you sing. Your voice called to me." His eyes glimmered with wonder and unbridled joy.

"Papa! Lady Ulla healed you. You're going to be all right!" Lukaz hugged his father, carefully resting his small head on the uninjured side of Cardin's broad chest. He raised a hopeful, tentatively optimistic face. "Can we still have the wedding? And live with Lady Ulla in Finistère?"

Cardin chuckled hoarsely. "Of course we will. But first, I'd like more water. Will you pour me a glass?"

Lukaz complied, proud and delighted to help his papa. While his father drank, Lukaz hugged Ulla. "I'm so glad your voice came back. Now you can talk again." He nestled his head against her stomach, his smiling face radiant.

Laudine and Esclados, wrapped in woolen cloaks against the Winter Solstice chill, kissed and hugged their son, overjoyed to see Cardin recover. Bastien, Gabrielle, and their children were next in wishing him well. King Guillemin thanked Cardin for saving Comte Ibarra, attributing the success of the Yuletide Treaty to his heroic chivalry.

Gaultier and Xabi congratulated *Basati* on the defeat of Andoni Zilar's assassins. Xabi handed Cardin the dagger that had been stolen behind the Drunken Crow in

Biarritz. "Got this from Gizon, Zilar's appointed assassin. Thought you'd like to have it back." A wicked gleam in his dark warrior eyes, he flashed a broken-toothed grin within his bushy beard. "Basati the Basque Wolf's blade."

"Come, everyone. Cardin needs rest. We'll see him again in the morning." Laudine ushered the relieved family members out the door, then turned to say goodnight to her son and Ulla. She kissed Cardin's forehead, wiping the dark hair away from his now cool brow. "*Dors bien, mon fils.* Sleep well, my son. Thank the Goddess you've come back to us." Gratitude and love blazed in her amber eyes as she beheld Ulla. "Thank you for healing my son." Wrapping her arms around Ulla's back, Laudine enveloped her in an affectionate maternal embrace. "If Cardin is hungry, there's plenty of soup left over from tonight's feast. On the hearth in the kitchen." She kissed Ulla's cheek. "Get some rest. See you in the morning."

Alone at last with the man she loved with all her heart, Ulla sat beside him on the bed and held his hand in her lap. She stroked the calloused skin with her thumb. "I had to reach you somehow. I could sense you slipping away." Her tender fingertips traced his face, and she leaned forward to kiss him softly. "I'd given you herbs…and sacred water from the well. I even placed healing crystals in the shape of a star around your body." She collected the glittering gemstones, tucking them back inside the pouch of the satchel near her chair. "But it wasn't enough. I needed more. And then it dawned on me. I could reach you in the darkness through music. I had to play my harp." She raised his hand to her lips and brushed his knuckles with a soft kiss. "I remembered the

Celtic Yuletide Carol I always sang each holiday season. The one you loved so much. As I strummed the familiar chords, my spirit soared to yours. Desperate to reach you, I found my voice. And sang you away from the darkness…back into the light."

Cardin pulled her to him, cradling her head over his chest. "I heard your voice. Felt your spirit call to me." He rocked her in his arms. "I fought my way back to you."

Content to be in his embrace, she lingered a few moments longer, then sat up and offered him more herb-infused water. "Are you hungry? Could you eat some broth?"

He grinned weakly. "I'm starved. Broth sounds really good."

She kissed him, her heart soaring like the chords she'd played for him on her harp. "I'll be right back." Slipping quietly from the room, she slid down the dim hall and into the dark castle kitchen. From the pot simmering over the banked fire in the hearth, she ladled a bowl of hearty broth and set it on a tray with a wooden spoon and a crust of bread. As she returned to Cardin's chamber, the waxing moon shone through the window, bathing the room in incandescent light.

The divine light of love which triumphed over darkness.

Thank you, dear Goddess, for answering my prayers.

And making my Yuletide wish come true.

Chapter 20

Twelfth Night Wedding

Cardin made a slow but steady recovery over the next few days leading up to the Yuletide festivities. His appetite increased, his color returned, and he was able to rise from the bed and walk to the alcove near the castle kitchen to share meals with his family.

With Vill on the nearby floor in front of the hearth, Ulla continued sleeping in the cot near Cardin's bed, changing his bandages and applying healing ointments as he regained his strength. "Let's go to your cottage," he'd said gruffly this morning, taking her hand and placing it against his hardened length. "I've recovered enough…"

"Soon, my love." She'd withdrawn her hand and kissed him softly. "Very soon."

Love, lust, and longing had danced deliciously in his dark green eyes.

Ulla had brought Lukaz to the castle stables for his equestrian training with Lord Quentin, Grandfather Esclados, and Uncle Gaultier. Now that Bastien and his sons Gunnar and Haldar had arrived at *le Château de Landuc*, the three of them had joined the riding lessons as well. "That's my Friesian, Kol," Lukaz had said proudly to his cousins as the boys watched the stable hand Argant brush the colt's shiny black coat. "He'll be ready to ride in three years. He'll hunt with me and my falcon Rask." Eyes widening in surprise as a sudden thought had occurred to him, he'd looked hopefully and expectantly up at Ulla. "Maybe Lord Chauvin could give Gunnar and Haldar each a peregrine, too. We could give them Viking names, like Rask and Finn." Nearly breathless with excitement, he'd suggested to his older cousins—who were obviously keen on Lukaz' brilliant idea—"Then we could all hunt together with our falcons in Finistère!"

"An excellent suggestion for a Yuletide gift," Bastien had remarked with a broad grin, resting his hand on Lukaz' shoulder as he eyed his exuberant sons. "Let's pay a visit to the Master of the Mews and have a look at his raptors."

As the three boys whooped with joy and departed with a jubilant, energetic Vill, Ulla smiled gratefully and returned to Cardin inside the castle.

****

The day before Christmas, as she had promised, Ulla and Lukaz—riding with Gaultier, Bastien, and several knights of Landuc and, of course, Vill bounding alongside—led the Archdruid Odin to the majestic oak in the heart of the forest where the two of them had found the enormous clump of mistletoe while hunting in the woods. Odin and his tribe of Druids distributed a sprig of *le gui*—sacred plant of the Celtic people—to the castle and to every household in the surrounding village. A cluster of mistletoe with fragrant white blossoms now hung in the doorway of *le Château de Landuc,* symbolizing the protection and blessing of the Goddess Dana and the beloved Forest of Brocéliande for the upcoming new year.

On Christmas Eve, with Gaultier's assistance, Cardin climbed the stairs with Ulla to join the entire family, King Guillemin, and Xabi in the private solar of *le Château de Landuc* for a sumptuous feast. They savored several courses, including a creamy chestnut soup, *velouté de châtaignes*, followed by fresh oysters, lobster, baked trout, roast boar, steamed vegetables, and Lukaz' favorite dessert—candied chestnuts called *marrons glacés.*

When the meal concluded, Ulla strummed her harp and sang her heart out, regaling the entire castle with a hauntingly beautiful melody, the same Celtic Yuletide Carol that had brought Cardin back from the darkness of death's doorstep and into the light of her healing love.

Christmas morning, before they joined the family in the private solar to exchange Yuletide gifts, Ulla changed Cardin's bandage and helped him don a clean woolen tunic. Pulse pounding in her temples, her mouth suddenly parched, she took his hand and raised it to her trembling lips. "I have a special gift for you," she whispered, resting his hand on her lower stomach. "I carry your babe. Our child will be born in late summer."

Panic warred with elation in his anguished eyes.

He's terrified because Charlotte died in childbirth. I have to reassure him.

"I've already given birth to a healthy son." Tears flowed as fond memories of her beautiful little boy Fjall filled her heart. "I'm young, healthy, and strong." She rose to her feet, taking his hands and running them up and down each side of her rounded bottom. "My ample hips are plenty wide enough…" she murmured, bending down to kiss him softly with a sensuous, seductive smile, "…to bear you several children." Ulla brushed a lock of hair from his furrowed brow. "Your mother will be my midwife. You'll see, my love. Everything will be fine." She grasped his hands and pulled him to his feet. "Come, let's join the others and give Lukaz his gift."

"Wait," Cardin said, crossing the room to retrieve a small package from a drawer in the walnut sideboard. He handed it to her with a shy smile. "I have a gift for you, too."

She untied the red velvet ribbon, unwrapped the gold-colored cloth, and opened the small wooden box. Her breath caught in her throat.

From a delicate golden chain, a pear-shaped, faceted ruby glittered in the morning sun.

"Before Xabi arrived from Biarritz, I had the castle jeweler craft it to match your wedding ring." He carefully lifted the necklace from the box and walked around behind Ulla. Pushing her long black curls aside to tumble over her shoulder, he fastened the pendant around her throat and kissed the nape of her neck. From a corner table, he fetched a mirror and held it up for her to see. "I thought you could wear it with your wedding gown. The ruby is red like your dress."

The deep scarlet gem was dazzling. As it lay against her skin, Ulla admired the exquisite jewel, caressing it with reverent fingertips. "It's perfect for my red velvet gown. I absolutely love it!" She rushed forward, threw her arms around Cardin's neck, and showered his smiling, bristled face with fervent, grateful kisses.

His hearty chuckle evolved into a guttural moan as he devoured her lips with his own. Parting them with the tip of his tongue, he delved deep, his ravenous hunger evident in the insistent hardness pressing against her belly.

Ulla withdrew from his intoxicating embrace, stepping back to catch her breath and adjust her kirtle. She exhaled slowly to compose herself before taking hold of Cardin's calloused hand and, with a whistle for Vill to follow, leading her betrothed out the bedroom door.

****

A blazing fire crackled in the enormous stone hearth. Through the elegant ogival windows of the eastern wall, morning sunlight filtered into the festively decorated room. Evergreen boughs entwined with holly, ivy, and berries adorned the elaborately carved wooden mantel above the enormous fireplace. The scintillating spice of cinnamon and cloves mingled with the tangy scent of citrus and the heady, earthy scent of mulled wine as Ulla, Cardin, and Vill entered the room.

She gestured for her wolf to lie by the door.

Upon an informal throne—an ornately carved gilded chair—a majestic King Guillemin, resplendent in a deep blue velvet cloak lined with ermine, sat between his royal hosts, Esclados and Laudine. Near the western wall, Gabrielle and Bastien were seated on a carved oak settee, their infant daughter Ylva in a nearby cradle, their three sons gathered on the floor. Gaultier and Xabi sat beneath the sunlit windows with a beaming Lukaz on his uncle's left, inside the entrance door. When he spotted Cardin and Ulla enter the solar, he proudly patted the settee he'd reserved for them to sit at his side.

While Jehan served the adult guests goblets of spicy mulled wine, Maëlys delighted the excited children with platters of sweetmeats and pastries as they impatiently waited their turn to open the Yuletide gifts.

In addition to peregrine falcons from the castle

mews, Gunnar and Haldar each received a finely crafted yew bow and a quiver of arrows. "Lukaz can give you both lessons when we return to Finistère." Bastien grinned at the young nephew he and Gabrielle had raised since birth. "He'll soon be as fine an archer as his father, Sir Cardin de Landuc, Captain of the Royal Archers for King Guillemin of Finistère." *And now that his illustrious father has returned, no one will call him a bastard ever again.* He met and held his younger brother's proud, grateful gaze across the cheerful room.

Lukaz tore open the silver cloth in which his gift was wrapped, thrilled to find a set of chain mail armor and a surcoat bearing the heraldry of Finistère. "It matches my new shield!" he exclaimed as he hugged his father tight, referring to the gift Cardin had recently given him for his seventh birthday.

"You can practice swordsmanship with Gunnar and Haldar. Next summer, when they train with Sir Lancelot and his knights at *la Joyeuse Garde,* you can go with them." *And when you return, a new sister or brother will welcome you home.*

Laudine loved the fur-lined cape Ulla had made for her. Ulla was immensely grateful for the assortment of essential oils and healing tinctures to add to her satchel of herbs. Cardin was majestic in his dark green woolen cloak lined with ermine, the symbol of his native Bretagne. Three-year-old Vidar adored his new wooden soldier. Gaultier appreciated the finely crafted leather sheath replacement for his sword. And Esclados admired his magnificent deerskin boots.

As Jehan appeared in the doorway to report that the Yuletide Feast was being served, King Guillemin stood and ordered the guests to wait, for he had an announcement to make.

"Before we gather in the Great Hall to celebrate this joyous occasion, I wish to present Sir Cardin de Landuc with a royal gift from King Philippe of France." He handed Cardin a rolled parchment tied with a black satin ribbon, sealed with wax, and embossed with the royal imprint of Paris.

Cardin sat down to unwrap the document, reading it with disbelief.

"Our sovereign monarch is most grateful that you safely delivered Comte Eztebe Ibarra to *la Tour Blanche*. Because of your valor, the Yuletide Treaty—the Alliance with Aquitaine—was successfully signed on the fifteenth of December at *le Palais Royal* on *l'Île de la Cité* in Paris." King Guillemin grinned heartily above his russet beard. "As a reward for your prowess, the Iron King Philippe le Bel bestows upon you the title of Vicomte de Saint-Briac, granting you one hundred hectares of land, including the peninsular oceanfront castle of *le Château Vert*. He bequeaths not only the enormous demesne, but six dozen knights to defend your castle and lands, and the generous sum of twenty thousand pounds of silver. As Vicomte de Saint-Briac, you will defend *la Côte d'Émeraude*—the entire Emerald Coast of northeastern Brittany. A most prestigious title of nobility and a most prestigious honor."

Cardin, stunned speechless, stared at Ulla, his mouth agape.

"Three valiant brothers defending King Philippe of France." With a majestic swoop of his regal arm, King Guillemin encompassed Cardin, Gaultier, and Bastien. "Sir Cardin, le Vicomte de Saint-Briac, defending the Emerald Coast of Bretagne. Sir Gaultier, of *le Château de Montmarin* in Biarritz, defending the French claims in Aquitaine. And Sir Bastien—my son-in-law and heir to the throne—defending the Breton kingdom of Finistère." He grinned at the crowd of jubilant faces congratulating Cardin on his title of nobility and the magnanimous royal decree.

Esclados, beaming with paternal pride, announced heartily: "Let us celebrate this glorious Yuletide gift as we feast in the Great Hall. Come, everyone. *Allons-y*!"

****

On January sixth, *la Fête des Rois*, castle guests gathered in the chapel to witness the Twelfth Night wedding of Lady Ulla de Montreuil and Sir Cardin de Landuc, le Vicomte de Saint-Briac.

Gold tunic shimmering in the candlelight, Cardin slipped the heirloom ruby on Ulla's finger. "With this ring, I thee wed."

The ruby pendant glittered at the base of Ulla's throat above the gathered bodice of her red velvet wedding gown. She slipped the gold band with a trio of ermine symbols—the heraldry of his native Bretagne—on Cardin's finger as she plighted her troth. *I am eternally grateful that the Goddess restored my voice. Not only did I reach him in the darkness with my song, I can now recite my vows.* "With this ring, I thee wed."

After the ceremony, exuberant guests congratulated the newlyweds and settled into the Great Hall for a sumptuous wedding feast. Lukaz, sitting between Cardin and Ulla, swallowed a mouthful of roast pheasant, washed it down with watered ale, and glanced apprehensively at his father. Worry shone in his innocent eyes. "Vill will come live with us, won't he?"

Cardin set down his mug of mead. "Of course he

will. And so will Nåde, Rask, and Finn." He winked at Ulla as he calmly reassured his troubled son. "One of Lord Chauvin's apprentices, Sir Yannick, is coming with us to *le Château Vert*—to become our Master of Mews. He'll take great care of our falcons. He's even got a peregrine for me." Bemused, Cardin met Ulla's gaze over Lukaz' head. "She'll need a Viking name, like Rask and Finn. Maybe you can help me think of one." The corner of his mouth curled up in a wolfish grin. "Lord Quentin is sending Argant to serve as our Master of Horse." He took another swallow of mead, observing Lukaz from the corner of his twinkling eye. "After all, we'll need him to teach you how to care for your Friesian. Because Kol is coming with us, too."

Lukaz jumped from his seat and hugged his father, his jubilant face crumpled in joy. "Thank you so much, Papa! I'll be able to see him every day. And bond with him. Like Lady Ulla did with Nåde."

"That's right," he agreed encouragingly, as Lukaz sat back down at his side. "*Le Château Vert* is only a day's ride from here. We'll be able to come visit *Mamie* and *Papi* often." He smiled at his parents, seated at opposite heads of the festively decorated table. "And your cousins in Finistère as well." Cardin grinned at Gunnar, Haldar, and little Vidar, seated between Bastien and Gabrielle, who cuddled the babe Ylva to her breast. "You'll train with my royal knights from Paris, and— once I've fully recovered—develop your archery skills with Lady Ulla and me." Pride and passion danced in his dark eyes as he held her gaze over Lukaz' small head. "Who knows? You might even become Captain of the Royal Archers at *le Château Vert.*"

"Perhaps you can come to Aquitaine one day. To

visit Xabi and me at *le Château de Montmarin*." With a great gulp of mead, Gaultier washed down a hearty bite of salted boar dripping with honey. He wiped his mouth with the back of his hand and directed his attention to Cardin. "With the generous gift of silver from King Philippe, you can finally pay off Itzal Baroja. Give me the hundred pounds you owe him. I'll bring it with me when we ride back to Biarritz and settle the debt for you." He downed the contents of his goblet and grinned at Xabi, seated at his side. "I can't wait to see *la dulce* Dolssa. I think about her every single day."

Xabi guffawed and slapped Gaultier on the back. "You're as besotted with her as I am with Euri. I'm going to marry her, you know. As soon as we return to Biarritz." He glanced at Cardin, his jovial expression becoming somber. "I wish you could be the best man at my wedding, Basati. But as the new Vicomte de Saint-Briac, you'll have your hands full settling into *le Château Vert.*" He raised his goblet in tribute, prompting everyone at the table to do the same. "To Cardin and Ulla. Congratulations on your Twelfth Night wedding, your title and oceanfront castle, and your land in *la Côte d'Émeraude.* To a lifetime of love and happiness."

Lukaz turned toward Ulla with large, imploring eyes. Hesitant and unsure, his voice was a timid whisper. "Now that you and Papa are married…can I call you *Maman*?"

She clutched Lukaz with loving maternal arms, gazing into the fierce, lupine eyes of her new husband. As a harpist began strumming the lyrical chords of the Celtic Yuletide Carol, Ulla's spirit soared on the uplifting melody like the unfurling wings of a swan. Cradling Lukaz against the bodice of her red velvet wedding gown, she kissed the top of his dark, sweet head. "Yes, you can, *mon fils*. You're my son now. And I love you with all my heart."

Thank you for purchasing
this publication of The Wild Rose Press, Inc.

For questions or more information
contact us at
info@thewildrosepress.com.

The Wild Rose Press, Inc.
www.thewildrosepress.com